DEAD IN THE WATER

THE DANGEROUS COAST OF FLORIDA
SUSPENSE SERIES - BOOK 1

CHASE WATERS

Illustrated by
NATASHA SNOW

Edited by
VALORIE CLIFTON

CONTENTS

Chapter 1   1
Chapter 2   13
Chapter 3   23
Chapter 4   35
Chapter 5   45
Chapter 6   55
Chapter 7   67
Chapter 8   79
Chapter 9   89
Chapter 10   101
Chapter 11   113
Chapter 12   127
Chapter 13   139
Chapter 14   149
Chapter 15   161
Chapter 16   171
Chapter 17   183
Chapter 18   195
Chapter 19   207
Chapter 20   219
Chapter 21   229
Chapter 22   241
Chapter 23   255
Chapter 24   267
Chapter 25   281
Chapter 26   289
Chapter 27   301
Chapter 28   313

Chapter 29   323
Chapter 30   339

About Chase Waters   347
Also by Chase Waters   349

CHAPTER ONE

"John," my partner, Sergio, said breathlessly, "I can't get the bleeding to stop."

I looked down at the young man as blood flowed from his belly and up to his chin. With every heaving breath, more of the viscous liquid oozed out. My partner knelt beside him with both hands lodged in his body cavity, but he couldn't stem the flow.

"We have to load him up," I said nervously. "He needs a few pints of blood immediately. We can't wait to stabilize him before getting him in the ambulance."

"I'm afraid to let go to lift him onto the stretcher," Sergio said nervously.

Another unit pulled up behind us. I let out a sigh of relief. We had backup.

"Over here," I call, but the guys climbing out of the truck ran in the opposite direction.

I swore under my breath. "Sergio, we have no choice. We need to get out of here."

The young paramedic nodded and maneuvered the patient, sliding the board underneath his body. Then, we quickly hoisted him onto the stretcher and into the back of the vehicle. Sergio jumped back in the ambulance in an attempt to stem the bleeding from the gunshot wound.

Then, I heard the shots ring out. I looked around but I couldn't see where they were coming from. Screams mixed into the commotion. People were in trouble, and there weren't enough EMTs to help them.

"You have to go," Sergio said, gesturing out toward the chaos. "You have to save those people."

I knew this, but I also knew that if I went into the mess, I could be seriously injured or killed. In five steps, I could be in my truck, on the way to the hospital. My partner and I could save the guy on the stretcher. But then, we'd be leaving the other victims.

"I don't want to," I said under my breath. I walked to the front of the ambulance and pulled the door handle, but it was locked. My bag of gear lay at my feet. It was as if I had no choice.

Slinging my bag over my shoulder, I ran straight

into the smoke. As I went, I saw bodies on the floor, but there was no chance I could save them. Without even examining them, I knew they were dead.

I found a woman curled up on the ground, her eyes pleading with me for help before she even opened her mouth.

"What's the matter, ma'am?" I asked, kneeling beside her.

She removed her hands from her chest to show a wound that went straight through her. I could actually see light on the other side of the injury. It made no sense that she could even be alive with such a severe wound.

"You won't make it," she moaned softly.

"Shh," I said. "Try not to talk."

"You can't save them all," she said, fighting for air. Bubbles of blood popped in the corners of her mouth. She didn't have much time left. I knew she wouldn't be making it into the ambulance.

"I can try," I replied.

She weakly shook her head. "Save yourself. Go."

I stood up and saw a gunman facing me. He was cloaked in dark tactical gear. He aimed his weapon at me, and before I could beg for my life, I heard a loud pop.

I sat up in bed, sweat beading on my forehead. I

took a moment to catch my breath, trying to shake the sick feeling I had from that awful nightmare. I had experienced many work-related nightmares during my time as an EMT, but none were that terrifying. At most, I had only ever woken to a sense of dread, not sweaty sheets.

I reached out for my girlfriend, but she wasn't in bed. I figured she had gone to the bathroom, so I reached for my glass of water on my nightstand and gulped it down. The bright red numbers on the clock told me that I had only been asleep for a couple of hours.

I lay back on the pillow, wiping my brow. I wondered if the people in my dream were people I had once helped. Typically, after going on a call, we would never really hear from the person again unless they took it upon themselves to seek us out and let us know that they ended up okay. Usually, we didn't know if someone lived or died unless we tried to find out. I rarely wanted to.

It wasn't that I didn't care, but I cared too much. I may expect the worse from an old person falling and breaking a hip, but the kid we perform CPR on after being pulled out of a pool is better off in my optimistic imagination.

If there was anything I took out of that dream, it was that I was so eager to turn and run when I was needed. If my dad had taught me anything, it was to stay and help until everyone was safe. But he was a military man, and there was no greater dishonor than leaving an innocent person alone to die.

I listened to the crickets chirp outside my window, waiting for my girlfriend to return to bed so I could relax. Marcie and I had been together for years, and she was a familiar source of comfort to me. Sometimes, just hearing her breathing was enough to lull me to sleep.

There was a voice in the other room. After careful consideration, I decided that Marcie was on the phone. But it was late at night. Her whole family lived scattered around Florida, so it wasn't as if she was waiting to speak to someone in a different time zone. I got out of bed and crept to the doorway to listen. She hated when I got into her personal business, so I remained incognito. It was hardly snooping, as she was in my home, talking to someone in the middle of the night when she would normally be in bed.

Suddenly, I could hear her voice loud and clear. I thought she must have been joking around with a friend, but her voice was much deeper and throatier than I had even heard it, even in the bedroom. If it was a joke, it had gone on for way too long.

"What am I wearing?" Marcie giggled from the

spare room. "Oh, I'm wearing my lace nightgown and no panties."

Unless she had changed, I knew that was a lie. I had watched as she pulled on a pair of boxer shorts and an oversized T-shirt. She wore the same thing every night.

"I can't take a picture right now," she said softly, "but I'll send one to you tomorrow before we meet up."

This got my attention. Marcie had mentioned that she was going to spend the night at her sister's house. She must have chosen that location because she knew it was the one place to which I'd never accompany her. Her family was fine and all, but her sister didn't seem to like me much.

"Well, I should get going. I'll talk to you soon."

Once I heard silence, I scrambled back to bed, rolling on my side. I slowed my breathing to a convincing rate and stayed still as she sneakily slid back into bed. I could tell that she was pleased with herself, having taken a secret phone call without my knowing.

I gave a fake groan and rolled over, wrapping my arm around her waist. "Did you get up? I had the strangest dream."

She paused. "I just got up to go to the bathroom."

"Okay," I said, knowing that I was catching her in a lie.

"Go back to sleep," she said before giving me a kiss on the cheek and rolling over to her side.

"Sure," I said softly, listening to her breathing. This time, it was not to soothe me back to sleep but to notify me of her incapacitation.

I wasn't a naturally devious guy. I had been raised by two upstanding citizens who'd taught me strong Christian morals. I was never to cheat, steal, or lie, as it was unbecoming of a young man.

Then, I'd decided that being a paramedic was no longer something I wanted to do. I'd worked very hard for a number of years, then burned out. I could no longer go to a job I dreaded going to. My fortieth birthday would be here before I knew it, and I didn't want to be a miserable old man. So, I decided to switch careers.

Private investigating wasn't as sexy of a career as one might think. While there were occasions where I could solve mysteries, most of my income came from finding guys who'd skipped on bail. A lot of my time was spent in my car, eating fast food while staking out a perp. In return for finding these people, I was cut checks just big enough to take care of rent payments on the home I shared with my girlfriend.

There had been many instances where I was hired to tail a spouse suspected of cheating. In almost every case, my client's suspicions were proven correct. I had files full of sneaky couples smooching in the park in the next town over, where they thought no one would ever recognize them. I had files of timelines and the whereabouts of the cheating spouse when he'd said he would be at work and was at his girlfriend's house instead.

I had seen it a million times, yet I was blind when it could be happening directly under my nose. My girl-friend was talking to someone when she thought I wouldn't hear her. I didn't want to betray her trust, but I thought it would be okay to snoop if she was on the verge of breaking mine. Of course, if I were just being paranoid, I would feel terrible for not trusting her. But I had a sneaking suspicion I was not wrong. With a little evidence to set me on the right track, I had a good instinct for these things.

Marcie had a tell for when she was asleep. Her legs would twitch as she entered the first sleep cycle. After a few twitches, I knew she was out. Stealthily, I crept out of bed again and reached for her phone, unplug-ging it from the charger. She had her phone password protected, but I had watched her carelessly type it in when she thought no one was watching. Even if I hadn't seen it, it wouldn't have taken me long to figure it out. It was the year she was born.

After typing in the four digits, I went straight for her text messages. If she was sending and receiving texts from strange men, she was doing a good job of deleting them. I couldn't find any correspondence.

Then, I went to her call log. There were several numbers that weren't named in her contact list, but the last entry was the only repeat offender. Someone in the area code had spoken to her almost every night of the week, sometimes more than once a day. I quickly memorized the numbers, then set her phone down as carefully as I had picked it up. Then, I typed the digits into my phone for safekeeping.

I would have to investigate in the morning. It wasn't as if I could go out and hunt this guy down in the middle of the night and not expect any repercussions. And I didn't want to give Marcie any reason to think I didn't trust her. I didn't, but that wasn't the point. If I could pretend like nothing was wrong, the investigation would go so much smoother than it would if she was trying to thwart me at every turn.

While my mind was racing, I was still pretty tired from being startled awake by nightmares. Because this happened frequently, my trick was to convince myself that I could table whatever thought was on my mind until morning. Finally able to relax to the point where I could close my eyes, I drifted off to sleep.

In the morning, I woke up early and went to my favorite coffee shop for an espresso and a blueberry donut. I was about to dive into my investigation of the mysterious phone number when I got a call from one of my regular clients.

"Godwin," I said shortly into my phone.

"Hey, John," the voice said on the other end. "It's Mikey. Listen, I've got a guy who's skipped on bail again. He's not terribly dangerous, but he's a sneaky son of a bitch. Are you available to track this guy down today? I'm willing to give you a bonus for this one."

I groaned and set my donut down on the napkin. I was more interested in my personal investigation than in any punk, but I had to pay the bills and keep up a good relationship with my regulars.

"Sure," I replied. "I've got nothing else to do today. Send me the file."

"Thanks, John," he said cheerfully. "Check your email in about five minutes."

I hung up the phone and wiped the crumbs from my hands onto my jeans. Now, I would have to table my suspicions about my girlfriend for at least another day as I searched the city for a wanted man. All the while, she was probably out doing the dirty with some hot young man. I knew I was nothing special in the looks department, but I thought we had a solid relationship. To think, I had spent years with this woman, giving her everything she ever needed, and she could keep secrets from me.

Alas, there was no time for heartbreak. I heard the

ping from my phone, a message telling me where I could find Jimmy West, a thirty-two-year-old white guy arrested for assault and a handful of weapons charges.

I tossed my empty coffee cup in the trash, wished the friendly barista well, and went back out to my dusty Buick. It was time for work.

CHAPTER TWO

I'm not sure what Mikey was on about because it took me relatively no time to find the bail-skipper. Using the information I was given, I talked to a few people who knew him. Luckily for me, Jimmy West was an asshole and had screwed over his friends and family at every turn. Even the most cop-averse friend had no problem giving me some information about where he might hide out. Hell, even his own brother told me where he had just been employed, but in return for Jimmy, he wanted me to take whatever money he had on him because he had some outstanding debts. I told the brother this was outside of my profession, but he could take it up with his lawyer when that time came. Eventually, this all led me to a meat-packing plant on the outskirts of town. I found Jimmy hiding among the chicken carcasses and pulled him out by his protective suit. By lunchtime, he was back in police custody, and I had a week's worth of rent in my pocket. It wouldn't last long, but it would continue to keep me afloat while Marcie was trying to decide what she wanted to do for a living in her next round.

As I drove back to Mikey's office, I started thinking about my plan of attack for dealing with my issue with Marcie. Since she was planning on going to her *sister's* house around seven, I would have plenty of time to figure out who this guy was. I could scope out his place, learn more about the guy, then sit and wait for her to show up. If I were correct, I would snap a few pictures of her as proof. Then, I figured I would have to kick her out of the house. The thought of doing this made me feel a little nauseated, though, so I blocked this image from my mind.

I was focusing so hard on the investigation aspect that I didn't even have time to think about how this was going to affect my personal life. It wasn't as if we were married, but Marcie and I had been together for a few years. She had lived with me for over a year, and in that time, we'd shared countless dinners, slept side by side, and talked for hours on end. She knew me better than anyone else in the world, and I thought the same about her.

She had been there for me when I changed jobs.

While she wasn't thrilled about my working as a free-lancer, she supported my decision as long as I wasn't so stressed out all the time when I came home from work. I made a little less than I used to, and the money wasn't always steady, but it was good enough for me. I didn't need much. She was the one who had greater needs.

And as much as I complained when we got into lovers' quarrels, I didn't really mind paying for her living expenses. She was a flaky and flighty woman, never content in her work. She'd be hired on as a sales representative at a mobile phone store, only to find that she hated sales and quit before her first commission check came in. Then, she'd work as a teacher's assistant at an elementary school, only to find that she didn't like kids that much. I understood what it was like to be discontented in one's work, so I never pushed her to stick with something long enough to receive benefits. I just went ahead and paid the bills, accepting help from her when she was able to give it. Otherwise, I let her borrow my credit cards and live rent-free in my two-bedroom condo. After all, when it comes to love, I didn't think it was right to provide her with an itemized statement of our joint financial contributions.

I had never had much of a love life, but I thought Marcie would really stick around. As my kinder friends would put it, I had been unlucky in love for much of my life. I'd had several long-term girlfriends who'd never really panned out. I was a decent guy, but I guess I wasn't enough for them. A girlfriend would talk about marriage and kids, and the moment I balked, she was gone. Or, one would want to quit her job and start a business, but when I expressed my concern about her loss of income, she'd call me unsupportive and bolt.

This wasn't to say that I was never at fault in these matters. I had been described as inattentive on more than one occasion. I was attracted to the high-maintenance types even though I was better suited for a low-maintenance girl. I had trouble with commitment in an official sense. I could date a girl for years with no issue, but once the prospect of anything permanent came into play, I froze up. I guess the thought of losing any freedom freaked me out. It wasn't like I did much outside of work, but I knew that I could if I wanted to.

"So, John, since you're back so early, do you think you can take on another case?" Mikey asked apologetically.

"What do you have?" I sighed, knowing that I wasn't really in a position where I could pass up a paying job.

He grinned. "This one's a bit of a rascal. And he's a bit dangerous, so you'll want to watch out. Have you started packing heat?"

I shook my head. "You know I'm not into that. If I

can't defend myself with my own two hands, I'd rather just leave and have the cops deal with it. I'm not an officer of the law."

"Suit yourself," he said, handing over his file. "It's probably better that way. I don't really trust any of the other guys to bring him in without accidentally killing him. We don't get as much money when that happens. Anyway, feel free to take your time with this one. We don't think he's a flight risk because he still has ties to the community. He just doesn't want to go back to jail."

"Got it," I said, giving Mikey a nod before walking out of his strip mall office. I got in my car and went to the hardware store. I had a few errands to run before getting back to work.

At the store, I purchased a few small recording devices, both audio and visual. I also bought a few motion sensors to wire into the recording equipment. It was something that one of my friends had taught me how to do when I'd first started working as a private detective. It would eventually keep me from having to sit and watch hours of footage for what could only be a few sound bytes.

Then, I drove back home where Marcie was in the bathroom, getting ready to go out for the day. Come to think of it, I supposed I rarely knew what she did during her days without work. Whenever I thought to ask, I accepted whatever answer she gave me without question.

While the shower was running, I quickly placed the recording devices in a few strategic areas. One camera went near the front door, while another went in the bedroom. I placed the tiny audio recorders behind picture frames in the hallway in hopes it would pick up any conversation in the area, in case the video was inconclusive.

When I was finished, I tapped on the bathroom door and peeked in as Marcie was drying her hair, wearing a towel. The whole operation took fewer than ten minutes. I was kind of an old pro at this by now.

"What are you doing home?" she asked, looking surprised to see me.

"I was in the area," I lied. "Hey, I was just going to let you know that I'm working a case tonight and I'm not going to be back until tomorrow morning."

"Oh," she said, looking confused. "Is everything alright?"

"Oh, sure," I said. "It's just going to take me out of town, so I'll probably rent a roadside motel room if I even get the chance to sleep. I'll probably just be staking someone out. I figured I'd let you know in case you had a change of plans or if you tried to call me."

"Okay," she said. "Will you let me know when you're on your way home?"

"I can do that," I replied. I went back into the bedroom and grabbed a duffle bag, picking up a few items I might want to have in case things went poorly at home. I grabbed a couple of changes of clothes, my phone charger, my toiletries case, and my laptop. I didn't want to be left without it if I couldn't go home. "Why do you ask?"

"Because I don't want you walking in here and scaring me when I'm not expecting you to be home, that's all."

"Yeah, I'll try to remember that," I said, kissing her on the top of her damp head. "See you tomorrow."

I grabbed an apple from the fridge and went back to my car. I wondered if I would find anything or if I would figure out about her transgressions elsewhere. Or, there was the possibility that my work was getting to my head and I was being ridiculous.

Nevertheless, I left my home feeling a little bit better about working on a real case instead of wasting time and money on personal affairs. I flipped through the file while static and classic rock came through my radio. When I had a starting point, I put my car into drive and cruised down the highway.

If there was anything I learned about myself between my two careers, it was that I liked to work a case. While I was an EMT, I liked arriving on a scene and figuring out what needed to happen first. I could see an unconscious guy on the sidewalk, and within minutes, I'd know if I needed to give him glucose or adrenaline. I could talk to a woman with abdominal pains and narrow down her problem within a few diagnoses. It wasn't always my job to diagnose the patient, but it helped if I had a reasonable idea of what they needed first.

It was the same thing with detective work. I could start with a bunch of leads and narrow them down into a few useful ones to solve the case. Similarly, I could start with nothing and work my way toward a lot of useful information. It all depended on what I was given. I just liked being able to observe and solve whatever problem came my way.

So, instead of worrying about what my partner of nearly three years was up to, I dove head-first into the case, letting my mind drift off to criminal activities, rather than the sexual ones that pervaded my happy memories of my girlfriend. Though I tried to fight it, flashes of Marcie kept appearing in my head.

Even though I knew things looked bad, I still couldn't help but think that I was making an error in judgment and she would be at her sister's house where she said she would be. Every strange piece of evidence could be explained away until it meant nothing.

For instance, the phone call could have been a joke with one of her friends. Taken out of context, I could see her being silly with a girlfriend and pretending she was talking to a lover. Or, she could have taken up a job as a phone-sex operator in an attempt to chip away at some of her credit card debt. Stranger things have happened.

Then, there were the repeat calls. If we continued with the phone-sex operator theory, it seems reasonable that she had a repeat customer. I wasn't exactly sure how those things worked, but it seemed possible. Or, someone she spoke with often, like her mom, could have changed her phone number and she had yet to add it to her address book. It was all within the realm of possibility.

Deep down, I probably knew these explanations were weak, but I had nothing else to hold onto. So, I doubled down in my denial and pretended as though nothing in my life would ever change and drove to my first destination. I didn't know what else I could do. I tried so hard not to let her potential infidelity distract me, but damn it, how could it not?

CHAPTER THREE

Matthew Vernon was a degenerate from all over the state of Florida. He drifted from city to city, trying to score or to sell. When the cops were too close, he'd bolt, finding a new place to set up shop. When he was finally arrested, he was lucky to only have a gram of coke on his person, though the DEA had his number for quite some time. But without enough evidence to convict right away, he'd been allowed to bail out and await trial. However, the trial date came and went, and Matthew was nowhere to be found.

From what my file told me, the guy was potentially responsible for a whole bunch of deaths up and down the state. This guy made a living selling bad drugs to junkies who couldn't say no to their addiction. He'd buy a small quantity of something pure, then add pharmaceuticals to them to strengthen the high. Then, he'd package it back up and sell it, telling people that he had the purest stuff on the block. A seasoned user would know their limit, but since the contents of the baggies were unknown, they'd unwittingly overdose.

It was the perfect murder because in general, no one really cared about what happened to these drug users. While it was sad for so many people to die, it was easy for law-abiding citizens to shrug their shoulders with apathy when the news told them of a new overdose death. Many believed that these drug users would die eventually. While this may have been true, it was also true that Matthew Vernon was directly responsible for their deaths. He played pharmacist to strangers on the street, lying to them about his product. These people didn't want to die—they wanted to survive until they could get their next hit. But when someone was discovered dead with a needle in their vein, no one investigated.

It wasn't just drugs, though. Vernon had quite the rap sheet, which baffled me as to why he was ever released on bail. The man had plenty of contacts with bundles of cash at their disposal. It would only take Matthew a few days of selling his special death blend to make up that money. I figured that was the plan all along. He wasn't a rich man, but he could come up with a lot of money in a short amount of time. If he could find himself so lucky as to make bail, he could hide in the shadows until his next arrest.

But I would always contest the judge's decision to set bail so low. not only was this guy selling bad drugs, but he had a tendency to be violent. And since he was a heavy user, he was unpredictable. I just hoped I'd catch him on downers rather than speed. I've dealt with heroin users and I've dealt with meth heads. It's a lot easier to put someone in a car if they can't keep their eyes open than if they can't keep still.

First, I traveled to a little podunk town, no bigger than five thousand people. With all of my teeth exactly where they were supposed to be, I was already out of place. Nevertheless, I climbed out of my car and walked toward a house with peeling yellow paint on the siding. I cleared my throat before knocking on the splintery wooden door.

I waited for a moment before I heard slow footsteps coming toward the door.

"Yeah?" a man with a weathered face grunted.

"Hi, I'm looking for Matthew Vernon," I said politely.

"What do you want with him?" he asked.

I pursed my lips, trying to figure out which line I

wanted to use with this man. I had a rotating script that I used, depending upon the situation.

"He's in a bit of trouble," I said. "I'm trying to help him, but I can't find him. This house was listed as one of his former addresses."

"No one can help that boy," the man said, his voice raspy. He pulled out a cigarette from his shirt pocket and lit it. "Besides, I haven't seen him in years."

"Do you have any idea where he might be?"

The man shook his head, his droopy blue eyes fixed on my car. "Nope. I can tell you he's not in this town. It's probably for the best."

I nodded. I had reason to believe this man. He was calm when he spoke, not nervous or distracted like liars usually were. I thanked him for his time and crossed the town off the list.

Back in my car, I rolled down the windows and moved on to the next location. This was a slightly bigger city than the last, an industrial town with a lot of blue-collar workers. Given the spread of the opioid epidemic in this part of the state, I thought it would be a good place to look. If I were looking to sell drugs, this is where I would come to make a cheap buck.

For this location, I would have to try another strategy. I looked too much like a cop in my polo shirt and jeans. I dug around in the backseat of my car and found a ratty t-shirt and a sweat-stained Marlins hat.

With dark circles under my eyes from a poor night of sleep, I thought it looked like I could be a drug user in need of some relief. In fact, if I had been one to use drugs, I might have sought some out to take the edge off. I kept wondering where Marcie was as I drove from town to town, trying to make enough money to support the two of us.

I found myself in a liquor store near the highway at the town's entrance. People sat outside on the bench, waiting for the bus or just waiting for something interesting to happen. The people who hung around didn't look like they had anywhere in particular to go.

I walked inside without greeting anyone, purchased a bottle of cheap malt liquor, and returned to the shop front. Cracking it open, I took a sip of the cold liquid and shivered. It didn't taste great.

With a grunt, I settled down on the curb, a few feet away from the front door. I took another sip, trying to look as though I was a proper alcoholic, though I couldn't really get blasted before going on a manhunt.

"I need something a little stronger than this," I grunted under my breath, but loud enough that the others could hear me.

There was no response from the crowd, but I figured they were the type to indulge in the substances I was hinting at.

"I've just got this awful back pain that won't go

away," I fished. "The doctors can't do shit for me. I lost my insurance when I lost my job. The guy who usually helps with this stuff has gotten himself locked up for possession, the dumbass."

I took another swig and waited for a response. Nothing.

"Say, I hate to ask, but does anyone here know someone who could help me out? I'm good for the money."

A young woman turned to me, glaring. "What are you talking about?"

I let out a weak laugh. "I'm not a fucking cop, if you think that's what I'm talking about. Someone told me about a guy whose name starts with a V, I think, but I don't remember. My memory's gone to shit these days."

"Vernon," a guy said in a gruff voice. He didn't turn to face me as he spoke.

I clapped my hands. "Yes, that's it. Where the hell can I find him?"

He shrugged. "I think he lives with his girlfriend. I don't really know," the guy said, getting up from his bench and climbing onto a bus before I could ask any more questions.

I pretended to chug the bottle in the paper bag and tossed it into the metal bin. Then, I hopped in my car and flipped through my notes again. The name of a girlfriend was listed on the fact sheet. I did a quick search in a database and found an address in town.

I don't know if it was because of the lead or if I had pretended to drink a little too much alcohol, but I felt a rush go through my system. I was one step closer to finishing this job. With each step, I got further and further into the case, taking me out of my constant concern that my girlfriend was cheating on me as I talked to the burnouts.

When I pulled up to the house, I was a little surprised to find that it was in a decent part of town. I don't know why, but in my mind, I figured I'd be walking through swampland to get to a dilapidated trailer or shack. Instead, I found myself at what looked to be a two-bedroom home with a neat lawn. It wasn't a spectacular home by any means, but it wasn't bad, either. It was perfectly ordinary. The perfect place to hide.

I checked my facts again to make sure I wasn't about to walk into the home of an elderly couple with no idea why a strung-out man was looking for someone. But it all checked out. Molly Green had ties to my guy a few years ago. Her record was completely clean, though. From what I could tell, she was a bank teller and just got caught up with the wrong guy. Who knows how people become attracted to each other? I didn't know Molly Green, but I wondered if we had more in common than either of us would have ever thought.

From what I could tell, they weren't together anymore. I wondered what kind of woman lets her junkie ex-boyfriend stay in her house after they've split, but I was sharing my home with a woman who talked to men in secret while she thought I was asleep. I really didn't have room to judge.

Seeing as she wasn't a criminal herself, I wasn't sure which approach to take with the ex-girlfriend. If she were a jilted lover with jealousy issues, I could go in and talk to her like an old friend as she spilled the beans about Matthew's location. Or, if she were on good terms with him, I'd pretend to be concerned about his wellbeing. Or I'd be someone looking to reunite with an old friend from jail. It all depended on the instinct I felt once I spoke to her. I could go from one plan to the next, just by making eye contact with a person and noting their facial expression.

However, I never got that far. The second my knuckles touched the door, I heard the sound of glass breaking. I peeked into the little window at the front of the door and saw a man and a woman in the midst of a fight. It took no time at all to identify Matthew with his dark hair and scarred face. He had an anger in his eyes that I recognized from the mug shot. I couldn't identify the woman, but it didn't really matter. Given Matthew's history, I had a feeling she was in trouble. I was not a police officer, so I didn't know if I was really allowed to be busting through the door, but as a bystander, I had to intervene before things got worse for the girl.

I turned the knob—the door was unlocked. I came in to find the perp beating the crap out of his girl. He had one hand grasping her long, sandy blonde hair in one fist and the other repeatedly punching her in the face.

I bolted in and rammed my body into Matthew, slamming him up against the wall. Molly screamed as I knocked him to the carpet and pinned him to the ground with my knee.

"Are you okay?" I asked the girl.

She nodded, her hands covering her bleeding mouth.

"Call the police," I wheezed.

She scurried off to the other room as Matthew squirmed underneath me.

"I can't breathe," he rasped. "You're killing me."

I panicked, loosening up my hold on him in fear that I would actually kill the guy and have to deal with the repercussions. I didn't want to go to jail after working so hard to peacefully track this guy down.

The moment I let up a little, the guy whipped around and scrambled to his feet. He swung a punch at me, but I dodged it, using the skills my father had taught me. He grabbed at me, but I fought back, pushing him into the wall. He rebounded, running into the kitchen to grab a knife from the block on the counter. Thinking quickly, I grabbed a kitchen chair. He took a stab at me, but I hit him in the side of the head with the chair, momentarily dazing him. His girlfriend returned, quickly snatching the knife away.

"Where are the police?" I gasped as I bound the man's wrists with zip ties I kept in my pocket for this very reason.

"On their way," she whimpered.

Matthew began to move, but I held him steady this time. I wasn't about to let him try to beat me again.

"Are you okay?" I asked Molly.

"Yeah," she said softly before giving me a sideways glance. "Who are you?"

I snorted. In all the commotion, I hadn't realized that I had basically broken into her house to go after my bail skipper. It had to be rather unsettling to have a stranger in her house, though I had just helped her out.

"I'm John," I said, nodding at her. "I'm a private detective. Your ex missed his court date."

"Oh," she said. "You're a bounty hunter. Well, you came at the right time."

The police pulled up to the house a minute later. I had to explain why I was there and give the police all of my information. Then, I waited around as Molly gave her statement. Finally, I was given a handshake by the police officers and I went on my way.

Mikey was thrilled when he heard my story. Immediately, he went to his desk and wrote me a check, adding an even bigger bonus than the one he'd promised me.

"John, I don't know what I'd do without you," he said, patting my back. "You're one of the best guys I've got. How is it that you always know how to get secrets out of people?"

I shrugged. "I guess I just ask the right questions."

"Well, whatever you're doing, keep up the good work. I don't have anything for you right now, but I'll be sure to give you a call when something pops up."

I shook his hand and returned to my car, eager to go home and rest. My body was tired and sore from fighting the drugged-up perp and I just wanted a hot shower and to lie on the couch for a few hours.

But those dreams were dashed when I went to my bed and found that it was already occupied. There, I found my long-term girlfriend on top of some guy I had never seen before.

I felt completely numb. In all the excitement with this latest job, I had completely forgotten about my own mystery at home. I didn't wait for Marcie to say anything but just turned around and walked right back out the door. I didn't have anything to say to her anyway.

arcie called a few times, but I wasn't in the mood to answer. I didn't want to sit there and listen to her try to explain herself. I had decided that the relationship could not go on any longer, even if she tried to make amends. I had a strong sense of justice and I didn't want her to win. I had already paid for her to live rent-free at my place for years. I paid all the bills and bought her food. I even let her use my money to buy things like clothes and nights out with her friends. The more I thought about it, the more I was positive that I had probably paid for her to get ready and go out with a lover while I staked out houses looking for other cheaters.

Finally, she left me a text telling me that she had actually gone to her sister's house because she didn't feel right being in my home when I had nowhere else to go. She was kind of right about that, but the point stung. I had been sitting in a diner, eating my feelings and waiting until I knew what to do. I was thankful that she understood that I didn't want to see or talk to her, and I hoped that she had removed all of her belongings.

I wrinkled my nose when I stepped foot into the house. There was something foreign about the smell. It wasn't necessarily bad, just unfamiliar. Another man had marked his territory in my home and in my girlfriend. I didn't want to live there anymore. It was the home I'd shared with Marcie. Without her, it wouldn't be the same.

Standing in my living room, I didn't know where to start. I didn't know where I would go, but I had to move. Marcie had more things in my home than I did. I could probably pack my belongings in a few boxes and leave, but Marcie would need a whole moving truck. I wondered if it would be easier to sign the lease over to her, but I knew she wouldn't be able to pay, and I'd end up paying the rest of my lease while she screwed whomever she wanted in our bed.

Without any system of organization, I just picked out things I would need in the future and shoved them in any storage containers I had. The contents of my dresser went into a battered suitcase. My books, knick-knacks, and random documents went into a duffel bag.

The framed pictures of the two of us went straight into the trash.

As I began to load my belongings into my car, I had a moment of panic. If I was going to close out all utilities to my place and end the lease, I would have to find a new place to live. That would be another deposit I'd have to pay while waiting to get my old one back. And if Marcie wasn't happy about the way I'd left her high and dry, I don't know if she'd keep the condo in its pristine condition so I'd get all the money back. There was just so much to do in a short amount of time. Meanwhile, all I wanted to do was lounge around in front of the television and feel sorry for myself.

One by one, I went through each utility service provider and canceled service to my place. In twenty-four hours, my place would be an empty shell of what it once was. I felt the same about myself.

Then, I called my landlord and had a long talk with him. I was friendly with the guy, but we weren't close. However, that didn't stop me from reluctantly telling him exactly what had transpired in the last day. He had been through a similar situation years before and sympathized with me.

"Say no more," he said as I begged him to terminate my lease early. "Consider it taken care of. If she takes too long to collect her things, I'll make sure she's out in a jiffy. Her name was never on the lease, so she has no right to be there without you."

"Thanks," I said weakly.

"No problem. Say, do you have plans for where you're headed next?"

"Not at all," I groaned.

"I've got some vacancies. I'll send the cleaners and have them ready for you to view in a day or two. Unfortunately, they're a bit smaller and not as nice as what you're used to, but they're not bad."

"That would be nice," I said. "Let me know when they're ready and I'll come take a look."

"Keep your head up, man," he said encouragingly. "I know how this thing goes. Eventually, you'll find that you dodged a bullet."

"I hope you're right," I said before thanking him again for his generosity.

There were more things I needed to do before moving out, but I wasn't in the mood. I went to the cupboard for a bit of whiskey, only to find that I was completely out of booze. So, I drove straight to my local watering hole for a few pints of beer to soothe my soul and take my mind off my cheating ex-girlfriend.

I found myself a lonely spot by the bar so no one would try to talk to me. Although, it wasn't as though that was usually an issue for me at this dive bar. No available woman wanted to chat up the thirty-some-thing ginger who was clearly not having a good day.

I initially thought that the incoming call I was receiving was from a cranky Marcie as she realized that my things were gone. Instead, it was an old friend I had met years ago, even before I was a paramedic. I hadn't heard from him in a long time, so I decided to answer and see what he was calling about.

"John, how's it going?" Max's warm voice said from the phone.

"I've been better," I said tersely. "How about you?"

"As always, I can't complain when I'm living in paradise," he said. "Unfortunately, I have a little problem and I'm not sure who to turn to for advice."

I sat up a little straighter on the barstool. "What kind of problem?" I asked, feeling mildly concerned. Max had always seemed to have it together.

"I guess life on the island isn't always as sunny as it may seem," he replied. "Someone died here a few days ago, and I think it looks fishy. The Florida police are supposed to investigate, but they tend to leave us alone. That's why people can get away with partying hard, if you know what I mean. Resort security usually keeps things in line, but it's beyond their expertise, and the Florida police aren't taking it seriously."

"Drugs?" I guessed. I had heard Max describe

what goes on in his new island home and it sounded like kids partying a little too hard.

"That's what the police say so they can close the case. I think it's more than that. I knew the woman who died, and she doesn't seem like the type to die from an overdose."

"A retiree like you?"

"No, she was a younger gal. She was the resort medic. The coroner said it was a heart attack, but she was fit and in her early thirties. That's why I'm involved now. Management asked me to step in until they found another resort doctor. I told them that I didn't really do that anymore, but I felt bad. They're really in a bind, and I'd hate for anything bad to happen to any of the tourists because there was no one to take care of them. So, I've been on-call for the past two days."

"What do you think happened to her?" I asked, interested in this developing case.

"No clue. I wonder if she had taken something different than what she thought it was."

"Bad drugs," I concluded. "I see it all the time."

"I knew you'd understand!" he exclaimed. "I think you're the perfect guy for the job."

I crinkled my brow. "Wait, what job?"

Max chuckled on the other end of the line. "If you're interested, I've got a gig for you. I want you to come down for a few days to investigate. You're the only person I know who's a private detective with medical experience. Check things out, enjoy the nice weather, and have a few drinks with me. Gather enough evidence to prove that something more serious is going on, and you'll help the island stay safe."

"I get that someone selling bad drugs is a problem, but do you really hate medicine so much that you're willing to bring me down for a few days to figure out what happened to this one woman? It's an isolated experience."

"Sure, but it could easily happen again. Besides, why wouldn't you want to come here for a few days of sun?"

I scoffed. "You've met me. You know I turn to a tomato in about twenty minutes of direct sunlight."

Max let out a hearty chuckle. "I guess I forgot about that. We have sunscreen here. What about if you brought your lady with you? I'm sure she'd have a great time. She doesn't have to do any dirty work. She can stay at the resort and drink frozen cocktails and lie out by the pool."

I cleared my throat. "She's no longer in the picture."

"Oh, I'm sorry," Max said, very apologetically. "I guess I haven't been keeping in touch. Time just doesn't work the same way out here."

"It's fine," I said. "It's a recent development."

"Well, all the better reason to come out here. I've already got a room at the resort ready for you. The resort owners are keen to have someone quietly investigate. You'll pay nothing while you're here, and you'll also be paid handsomely if you can give any sort of closure to the situation. I'd say it's worth a shot."

I chewed on my fingernails. This job was sudden, and I had too much going on to properly think about it. I could take other jobs at the drop of a hat, but that was only because they required a short drive to reach my location, and I was often home by suppertime. Max wanted me to go to an island resort for a few days to investigate a murder. I snooped on cheating spouses and bail-skippers. This was beyond my expertise.

"I don't know, Max," I said. "I have a lot going on here at the moment. I have to move out of my old place and find a new place to live. I'm exhausted and kind of strapped for cash at the moment. My future is just so uncertain right now, and I don't know if it's a good time to be investigating potential crimes of this nature."

"It sounds like it's the perfect time to do such a thing," he replied.

My phone began to buzz as I thought about Max's offer. It was Marcie. I imagined that she wanted to talk to me about how we would move forward, and I wanted no part in that. I would be forced to tell her to her face that I was completely cutting her off, inevitably leaving her in a bad place. She would certainly take that hard, and I didn't want to face her wrath. I truly loved her, but she had an intense personality that came out when things didn't go her way. I was afraid that if she talked to me, I would get sucked back under her spell. I didn't want either of those things to happen.

"What if I bungled the investigation?" I asked after silencing my ex's call. "I'm technically an amateur at this."

"Then at least you tried. We need someone who can collect information without freaking the visitors out. A heavy police presence is not good for business. I don't really care that much about the resort owners, but there are a lot of good people who work here who would be displaced if the place went under. And I don't really want to pack up and leave if it does. Mostly, we just want to know why an employee died and prevent it from happening to anyone else. If it was really a heart attack, fine. But I have a feeling it's something more."

"You just want to write about this in one of your books," I said.

Max laughed again. "Maybe one day. For now, we just want some closure. Think you can help us out?"

The more I thought about it, the better the whole

thing sounded. I could successfully avoid Marcie while working in a new environment for a few days. And maybe the time away would be good for me. I wasn't usually one for beach vacations, but it was free and I needed a place to crash for a few days.

"Okay," I said, hearing the exhaustion in my voice. "I'll come out and investigate for you."

"Awesome!" Max said. "I'm excited to have you! Now, do you think you can meet me at the pier at eight tomorrow morning? The boat is coming in to pick up a few supplies and I'm coming along to greet you."

"Sure," I replied. "I'll see you then."

I hung up my phone, finished my drink, and paid my tab. Now, I would have to repack for a few days on an island and find a hotel to check into so I could get some proper sleep before starting my new job.

I pulled out my phone and fired off a quick text message before turning it off completely.

I'm going away for a few days. I terminated my lease and you have twenty-four hours to remove your things. Don't bother trying to contact me. Maybe we can talk in a few days. Maybe not. We'll see.

CHAPTER FIVE

leary-eyed from a poor night of sleep, I waited at the pier for a boat to turn up. I imagined some sort of cargo ship would arrive to pick up supplies to fuel a luxury resort a stone's throw from the Florida Keys, but instead, a speed boat popped up on the dock.

Max waved wildly at me from the seat in the back. He was a portly, middle-aged man who was almost entirely bald, save for a half-circle in the back of his scalp. His skin was tan and leathery, his naturally golden complexion further baked in the hot sun. He wore a jovial expression on his face that suggested to me that he had already had a cocktail this morning. From what he had told me about his time on the island, his diet was made up of rich, all-inclusive foods and alcohol. As someone who'd once made a living telling others how to live a healthy life, he didn't seem to buy into that advice. This was a man who was doing whatever he could to squeeze some enjoyment out of life before it was over. He was only a few years over fifty, but he lived in a way that would make one suspect he didn't have much time left.

You wouldn't guess by the look of him in his oversized floral print shirt and cargo shorts, but Max was once a highly-respected physician and educator. He had an incredible knowledge of the human body and modern medical practices, but he never seemed to enjoy the practice aspect of the career. So, he'd switched tracks and taught at the University of Miami Medical Center.

That's where we first met. I was a student for a hot second and he was my instructor. Neither of us were meant to be where we were, but we both tried to stick it out as long as possible. His problem was that he liked to learn about the intricacies of medicine but didn't want to get his hands dirty and work in the field. My problem was that I only wanted to work in the field but didn't have the mind for details or the motivation to study. It was no surprise that in less than a semester, I was out of school and Max had retired early at the age of forty-five and moved to an island resort.

Would both of us be better off if we'd just managed to stick to medicine? Perhaps. Would we be miserable?

Absolutely. I may be scrambling for jobs and Max may be drinking his liver to death, but we were both in better places than we were fifteen years ago.

"It's nice to see you again," Max said. "When was the last time we met up?"

I thought for a moment. "Probably your daughter's wedding," I said.

"Has it been that long?" he said, puffing out his cheeks. "Wow. You look good."

"Don't lie." I laughed as I climbed onto the boat. "Time hasn't been kind to either one of us."

Max smiled. "There's that sunny personality I enjoy so much. Are you ready to go?"

I frowned. "I was expecting a bigger boat. I thought you were getting supplies."

Just then, a man walked over with two boxes and handed them to the driver of the boat, who stored them in a compartment below deck.

"There we go," Max said with a nod.

"That's it?" I asked.

"Now that I'm in charge of the hospital, I want to make sure we have everything we need in case of another mysterious death. I ordered your basic overdose antidotes. You never know what you're going to find on the island."

"Lots of drugs?" I asked.

"You have no idea. For the most part, it's pretty

under the radar stuff. Paradise Key can be a pretty wild place. We get a lot of spring breaks and bachelor parties. It's an upscale place, so rich kids manage to bring in all sorts of pills and powders. For the most part, it's done without incident. Every once in a while, you'll get an idiot who did a little too much acid and is freaking out, but that's pretty rare. Security won't bother anyone about it unless they're being an idiot. That's why there's not much of a police presence around our parts. Anyway, I thought it would be best to have some extras on hand in case my suspicions about bad drugs are correct."

"Smart," I said as the boat started to rumble. As we cruised toward the island, Max yelled fun facts and stories into my ear. As a resident for the past five years, Max knew all the regulars and delighted in telling me everything that had happened while living there.

"I'm telling you, once you live here for a while, you're not going to want to return to the mainland—not even for a hurricane."

I rolled my eyes. "I'm sure I'd evacuate for a hurricane."

He shook his head emphatically. "No, you don't need to. This place is built as sturdily as could be. I'd rather stay in the resort than risk it in Miami. Honestly, it's that safe. There was still a lot of damage from the storm a few years back, but no one was harmed. At the time, it was scary as hell to see that much water splash up on shore, but we were fine. Besides, we were safe in our resort while people were acting like animals on the mainland. I'm telling you, this is the place to be."

"If only we could all afford to vacation every day," I said under my breath.

"I'm sure you could get a job working security. Some of those guys party harder than the tourists on their off days."

I pretended to entertain the thought, though I knew that my stay on the island would be short-lived. Max seemed to think that the party atmosphere would bring me joy, while I had the impression that it would only make me feel lonelier.

As we made our way to the island, I started to feel a little queasy. The more I thought about it, the more I realized I had no idea what I was doing. I was a guy who followed pretty comprehensive clues and used my muscle to take down bad guys. I was basically like a bouncer in a club, but for the criminal justice system. I also wasn't a medical examiner. I was a medical school dropout-turned EMT-turned private investigator. I had no real formal training in homicide investigation. If this death was really more sinister than a heart attack, then there should be real professionals involved. By showing up and pretending to be useful, I was giving people the illusion that they were safe to continue partying.

"Almost there," Max said, likely noticing that my pale skin had gone green. When we got to the dock, I felt relieved. On wobbly legs, I followed Max down the boardwalk, straight to the bar.

"Oh, I really don't feel like drinking," I said.

"I just need to get the key to the golf cart," Max said, reaching his hand across the bar. He seemed like he owned the place. I guess if you pay for a room for long enough, you kind of do.

Key in hand, he walked me over to the cart and punched the gas. I wondered if he was sober enough to drive.

"Let me take you on a little tour," he said. "Everyone's out this time of day for lunch on the pool deck. The weather is just right this time of day. It's warm, but there's a nice breeze coming off the water."

He closed his eyes for a second and took in a deep breath through his nose. I wished he'd keep his eyes on the road.

"Okay, there's Daniel Bergeron. He's the eldest of the Bergeron brothers. Those are the guys who own the majority of this place. They also live here for most of the year."

"What's he like?" I asked, nodding at the dark-haired man. He reminded me of a vampire. His dark hair was slicked back neatly, exposing his pale face. I watched as he gripped a coffee cup with his long, slender fingers. He had a pinched expression on his face, perhaps from stress. Daniel was slim but not skeletal in his khaki trousers and dress shirt.

"Oh, he's a good guy, but he works too hard. He's got other brothers here, but he always looks so damn tired all the time. He lives on an island but is as pale as you are. When you meet him, I bet you'll think he's a bit cold and standoffish. When you get to know him, you'll find that he's kind. He's just kind of uptight at times."

We drove on, passing by beautiful flowers and perfect hedgerows. Grass clippings floated along the immaculate roadway as we zipped along. Max slowed down a little bit and yielded to a man walking in the opposite direction.

"And that was Sebastian Bergeron," Max said out of the side of his mouth after we passed the man.

"I can tell they're brothers," I said, noting their identical height and build.

"Sebastian's a few years younger," Max said. "Though the grey hair around the temples ages him. I've always wondered if Daniel dyes his hair. I guess I'm not one to talk about bad hair." He laughed, rubbing his bald head.

"Is he equally serious?" I asked.

"The only thing he's serious about is women." Max laughed. "He has quite the reputation of sleeping with

everyone on this damn island. Hell, I've even accidentally walked in on him with some college-aged girl.
Well, I hardly call it walking in on him—he was in the
hot tub."

"So he uses his resort as a way to choose his
women? I can see the appeal for a guy like that. They
arrive, he gets what he wants, and then they go home.
It's kind of brilliant."

"From what I've heard, it's not just the visitors he's
after," Max said with a cheeky wink.

"Any more brothers?" I asked.

"Yeah, that's Jamie," Max said, pointing down to
the beach. I scanned the horizon and only saw one guy
running along the water. He was a hulking man, almost
as if he were an amateur bodybuilder.

"That guy?" I asked in disbelief.

"I know. He looks like he was fathered by someone
else," Max joked. "But he's a lot like his eldest brother.
He's not as hard-working and cold, but he is pretty
quiet. He's a total jock, but I think he's secretly a little
academic. Those brothers are a mystery in themselves,"
he said, "but it doesn't take a detective to figure them
out. I'm waiting for the perfect opportunity to write
about them."

I watched as the blond man jogged along the beach
without his shirt, his skin golden brown. I couldn't help
but envy these brothers. They were tall, handsome,

and rich, and I couldn't help but feel as though they got everything they wanted out of life.

"Jamie's in a failing marriage with a total bitch of a wife. He's a good guy, so I feel pretty bad for him."

"What's so bad about his wife?" I asked.

Max wrinkled his nose at the thought. "Cara? She's never been nice to me. Hell, she's never been nice to any of the regular staff here. I think she's a spoiled brat who thinks she's better than us. Anyway, I don't like to speak ill of people, so I'll leave it at that. Just don't be surprised if you meet her and she doesn't treat you so kindly."

"Got it," I said. "What's this place?" I asked as we pulled up to a small white building. Several golf carts were parked out front, just like ours.

"You have to check into your room," he said, stopping the cart. "Just go in there and tell them your name. Someone will take you and your bags up to your room. Settle in, and then meet me down at the bar. You'll want a drink before our next task."

I hoisted my backpack over my shoulder and got out of the cart.

"What's our next task?" I asked nervously.

"We have to examine the body."

I blinked, my mind going blank. "It's—it's still here?"

He nodded. "Between you and me, it's in the

refrigerator. It's probably best if you don't repeat that to any guests. It's in a separate area, but you know how people are about health codes."

I gave a nod. "Got it. When do you want me to go to the bar?"

"Give me an hour," he said, taking the brake off. "See you then."

I watched as Max drove off before heading into the office. I had thought it when I got on the boat, and I was thinking it again—I was in too deep. If it weren't for my cheating ex-girlfriend, I'd probably be at home, waiting to get a call from Mikey. Instead, I was preparing to check into an island resort, only to prod around a dead woman in an industrial refrigerator. It hardly felt like a promotion.

_____

CHAPTER SIX

After taking a moment to unpack and wash up, I lay on my bed in my room and tried to analyze the tiny pieces of information I had received. If we were dealing with a drug overdose or poisoning, a list of every guest who'd stayed in the last week or so would need to be collected. From there, I would have to take witness reports and figure out who was peddling drugs, and to whom. Once toxicology came back, the type of drug in the deceased's system may give me a better idea of what happened.

I was eager to speak with the brothers and see what they knew about the situation. I figured that at least one of the three men would know the goings-on of this resort. At the very least, they should know their own medic fairly well.

When I got to the bar, Max was already guzzling a

Bloody Mary from a highball glass and eating a greasy-looking egg sandwich. It was astonishing that they'd named the island lush the interim healthcare provider, but I guess they didn't really have any other options.

Feeling a little better from the boat ride, I ordered a bowl of fruit and a rum and Coke. I didn't want to eat anything heavy before looking at a dead body. I wasn't squeamish, but sometimes, the smells of death could be a little too much to bear.

"So, can you tell me what the general mood is like around here?" I asked, pulling out my notebook. "I understand that this place is somewhat hedonistic on a good day, but what's it been like since the death?"

Max nodded. He seemed to have a good feel for the ins and outs of this place. I was starting to think that if he weren't such a drunk, he'd be able to solve it himself.

"There's definitely a different feel around here," he replied, looking forlornly toward the sea. "You know, this kind of thing never happens here. Sure, we get some freak accidents every once in a while, but never a death. Dawn had been here for a few years now and was pretty well-liked. I know the two of us sat down on several occasions to talk shop. If I remember correctly, she was a registered nurse or a physician's assistant, or something like that. She had gone to school for a long time, worked hard for a few years, burned out, and came here. She was still young and wanted to have a little more fun before she got too old. Of course, I'm living proof that you can never get too old for this kind of lifestyle."

I smiled politely. I didn't want to break the news that he was probably too old for the partying lifestyle.

"What was Dawn like? Did she get along well with others, or did she have enemies?"

"Dawn?" he asked. "Oh, no, she was an absolute sweetheart. Everyone loved Dawn. She was one of those people who just exude love and positivity. That's why everyone's taking her death so hard. It feels like a shining light went out. I know she was close to the Bergeron brothers, and that's why they've been so down in the dumps the past few days."

"Was she a drug user?" I asked.

He shrugged. "Sure. But you have to remember, just about everyone here uses something recreationally. She was no junkie, but she knew how to party."

"If you had to guess, what kinds of drugs would she be more likely to take?"

Max thought for a minute. "Weed, Ecstasy, cocaine. Maybe something pharmaceutical like Xanax. Acid, if it's a wild party. That's probably about it."

"Got it," I said, writing a list in the margins. Some of these drugs could easily be tainted, and others were easily overdosed on. If she was using coke and did too much or it was cut with something stronger, then I could see where heart malfunctions could come into play. But if toxicology only showed weed in her system, then we could assume that foul play was involved or that she had underlying health problems.

"Have the brothers said anything to you?" I asked.

Max shook his head. "Hardly. I gave all them my sympathies. Jamie actually teared up when I spoke with him. I think he's probably the most sensitive of the bunch, as the youngest. It's been devastating for them, absolutely devastating."

I chewed on the inside of my cheek. Clearly, these brothers had a close connection to their employee. Perhaps they would have a better idea of what she might have taken.

"Did she have any known pre-existing conditions?" I asked Max.

"None from her medical records," he replied. "Of course, that doesn't mean that there was nothing there. As you know, many congenital heart defects go undiagnosed—that is, until something goes wrong."

"Right," I replied. "Overexertion or drug use could bring the problem to light."

"Exactly."

"Any other rumblings?"

Max gave a wry smile. "Always."

"Anything that's worth a deeper look? Well, I guess it doesn't matter. I'll take anything at this point."

Max leaned in a little closer to me. "I heard that Dawn slept with a lot of guys here."

"So? It sounds like that's the norm for just about everyone here."

"Yeah, but I think this is a little different. I heard that she was almost exclusively into the Bergeron brothers."

"At the same time?" I asked in disbelief.

"No, no, I don't think so," Max said quickly. "I think they had some sort of arrangement with her. They each took their turn."

"Really?" I mused, jotting down that note under *Unverified Rumors*.

"That's just what I've heard," he said, shrugging his shoulders. "Look, I think it's time to see the body. I've got some supplies right here," he said, holding up a bag. "It's hardly standard procedure, though."

"Let's get it over with," I said, draining the rest of the drink. I followed Max to the restaurant to view the body of a young woman taken before she had the chance to really enjoy her youth. I felt for her. Five years ago, I wasn't remotely settled down. Even after a career change, I still felt confused and restless at times. She had come to the island to enjoy herself, and now the poor thing was dead.

When we got to the storage refrigerator, I was surprised to find that we were not alone. As we opened the heavy door, I saw a woman in a lab coat crouched down beside the sheet-covered body.

"Who are you?" Max asked rudely.

She turned and scowled at Max. "I should ask the same about you. I'm from the Miami-Dade Coroner's Office."

"I'm Dr. Max Diaz. I'm the interim medic at the resort," he said proudly. "My private investigator has come to look at the body."

"We're taking it back to the mainland," she said coarsely. "There's really nothing more to investigate. I've already sent blood samples back to my office, and there is no indication that any substance was involved. It's pretty clear it was cardiac arrest."

I tapped my foot impatiently. "What all did you test for?"

"Any reasonable substance," she said grouchily. "Really, it doesn't do us any good to have other parties messing with the deceased—unless you have the permission of her family."

Max sighed loudly. "I was close to her. Can I at least have a minute alone to say goodbye?"

The medical examiner rolled her eyes. "Just don't touch the body. I have to talk with the owners, but I'll be right back."

"Yes, ma'am," Max said, watching as the heavy

door closed behind her. He wasted no time in unzipping his pouch and revealing several syringes.

"Take blood from the same place they did," Max instructed, pointing to Dawn's uncovered arm.

Carefully, I drew the plunger back until the syringe was filled with blood. Then, I deposited small amounts into several vials that Max closed with a rubber stopper.

"What are you planning to do with these?" he asked.

"Remember Carlos Vega? He works in Toxicology now. I think he'd be willing to do a favor for an old friend."

"Ah, yes, your old ambulance partner," Max recalled. "How's he doing?"

"Better than me. He's at the lab in the University. He's got a wife and a couple of kids. He's living the dream."

Max nodded. "One of the dreams. Are you going to have him run your standard drug panel?"

"Yeah, just to be safe," I said. "Maybe I'll give him some details and see what he thinks. He'll know more about this than I do."

After the blood was carefully stowed, I looked over the rest of the body, latex gloves on my hands. The last thing I wanted was for my DNA to come into question. I had a good alibi, as I wasn't even there, but I still didn't want to be called away from my work to clear things up.

From what I could tell, there was absolutely no bruising, no cuts or abrasions to be seen. Her body was stiff and cold but in remarkably good shape. She was not beaten or battered in any way, nor did she suffer from any kind of accident.

"Where was she found?" I asked.

"In her room. It appears that she vomited in her sink before retreating to her bed, where she passed away. But nausea and vomiting are not uncommon in patients suffering from a heart attack."

I took a step back and rejoined Max, who was putting his supplies back in his bag. "What if the medical examiner is right?"

He shrugged. Could be. I guess we'll know for sure when your samples come back from the lab. Or, we can wait until we have proof of a heart defect."

The woman from the coroner's office returned, this time with Daniel in tow. He flinched upon seeing the uncovered body of his medic. I quickly pulled the sheet back over her head.

"I told you not to touch the body," she said crossly, glaring at Max.

"I needed to see her for closure," Max lied. "This death has been hard on our little community."

"He's right," Daniel said morosely. "Dawn was a

great employee and a good friend. We're all going to miss her very much. Of course, we'll be paying for her funeral expenses. Her poor family must be absolutely gutted right now. I can't imagine losing a family member like that."

"It's a pain that never goes away," Max said sympathetically.

"I think it's time for you to be leaving," the medical examiner said through gritted teeth. She really did not like our being there. I kind of understood where she was coming from. After all, she was the professional trying to do her job. She had to travel quite a way to deal with this death, and she probably wanted to get back to her office and get to work. Meanwhile, amateur sleuths were meddling with her subject, trying to tell her, a trained professional, what had really happened.

"I'll walk you guys out," Daniel said, nodding at the ME.

"I'm sorry for your loss," I said awkwardly.

"Thanks," Daniel replied. "Did you find anything that she didn't already tell me?"

"I don't think so," I said sheepishly. "It's kind of hard to tell without the full results of the autopsy. I think we can rule out anything violent, though. It really just looks like she fell ill and keeled over. It's rare for that to happen to someone young and healthy, but I guess it happens from time to time."

"That's unfortunate." Daniel sighed. "It's bad enough to lose a beloved staff member, but now I'm worried that the news is going to catch wind of this and scare customers away. However, the examiner's testimony should put everyone at ease if it really was just a sudden death. It's not great for closure, but at least it's not murder or anything like that."

"Did you see Dawn on the night of her death?" I questioned.

Daniel shook his head. "I ran into her earlier that day as she went to lunch. I didn't stop to chat. If I would have known I wouldn't get another chance to, I absolutely would have."

I studied Daniel's face when he spoke. His words were full of emotion, but his face was tense and devoid of feeling, as was his voice. However, it could be a defense mechanism. Many tough men put up walls in the face of great emotional turmoil.

"I have to get back to work," Daniel said after clearing his throat. "I'll see you two later."

Max looked at his watch and yawned. "I actually have an appointment at the moment. Can you entertain yourself?"

I frowned. "What do you have to do?" I was under the impression that Max was only on call.

"I have a nap scheduled." He grinned. "I'll see you later."

I rolled my eyes and headed back toward my room. I needed to get in contact with Carlos and let him know that some samples were headed his way.

Along the way, I heard shouting, so I peeked around a wall to investigate. In a cabana, I saw Sebastian with a skinny blonde woman who fit Max's description of Cara perfectly. She wore a swimsuit cover wrapped tightly around her thin waist and had bracelets dangling off bony wrists. She wore giant sunglasses that kind of made her look like a bug, but she was still undeniably attractive.

I couldn't tell exactly what they were arguing about, and when I got into a better position to hear them, it stopped. Peeking around a palm tree, I realized they were getting hot and heavy with each other. Embarrassed, I quietly jogged back to my room, hoping no one had seen me spying on the couple. Whatever the issue was, it was clear that it was just a little lover's spat between a man and a woman. I had certainly experienced plenty of those in my day.

Back in my room, I flipped through my notes and suddenly remembered something I had totally forgotten about Max's rundown on the Bergerons—Cara wasn't married to Sebastian. She was married to his brother!

CHAPTER SEVEN

As I ate dinner alone in the dining room, I tried not to make eye contact with Jamie Bergeron. Just hours ago, I had witnessed his wife cheating on him with his brother. It wasn't my place to bring it up, as I had only known the family for less than a day, but having been fooled by a cheater before, I wanted him to know what was going on behind his back.

Unfortunately, he approached me as I was about to get up and sneak back to the bar in search for Max.

"Hey, man," he said, slapping me on the back. I could tell instantly that the man was wasted. I wondered how many it took for such a big guy to get drunk. He had to have been around six foot six and two hundred and fifty pounds or so. I had enjoyed a few beers with my dinner, but I was nowhere near his level of inebriation.

"Hi, how's it going?" I asked meekly. I hadn't been formally introduced to Jamie but had already learned more about him than I felt I should know.

"Welcome to the resort," he slurred. "Would you have a drink with me? I normally don't fraternize with the guests, but you're an extra-special guest."

"Oh, sure," I said, not wanting to be rude. Besides, I had learned that it was best to learn about a person while they were mildly intoxicated. I got more truth and less bullshit that way.

He sat down at my table and waved the waiter over. "Can we get a pitcher?" he asked.

I bit my tongue. I wasn't in the mood to get sloshed, not with all the work I had to do. But I didn't want to make an enemy on my first night.

"And some water?" I added. The waiter scurried off, taking my empty plates with him.

I could hardly believe that Max thought Jamie was quiet. From the second he'd eyed me, he came to my table to socialize. Perhaps this would be the only opportunity I'd ever get to speak with him.

"I'm sorry about what happened to your medic," I said. It had become custom to start each line of questioning this way.

"Thanks," he said, looking down at his empty glass. "It's been hard on everyone. It's hard to talk about."

"I understand," I said softly. "This place is beautiful."

"Ever since we were kids, it was our dream to build our perfect getaway," Jamie said, perking up a little. "Back then, we just wanted a fancy tree house. But as we got older and understood the benefits of owning real estate, we decided to pool our funds and make it a reality."

"That's great," I said. "What exactly do you do here?"

"I'm on the board," he said. "Day to day, I do some management. I'll help with new hires or issues with the staff. We have managers for these things, but they report to me if they have problems. Sometimes, if we're really swamped, I'll just grab a lawnmower or leaf blower and tend to the lawn."

"Really?" I chuckled. "I'm sure there aren't many resort owners who are willing to do the dirty work."

"Oh, I don't mind," he said, waving his hand. "I like to work with my hands. Gardening is one of my hobbies."

"Huh," I said, amused by this. For such a buff guy, I figured he spent all day at the gym. Now, I was learning that he liked to plant flowers. I realized I was making assumptions about these people without the facts to back them up.

"I actually have a greenhouse here," he said. "It's something I like to do in my free time. Some of the ingredients for our dishes come from there. You had the pad Thai tonight, right?"

I nodded.

"The cilantro on top came from my greenhouse," he said proudly. "I think some of the chilies did too. My brothers are fine with it because it helps cut costs in the kitchen. That way, we don't have to pay to get certain things shipped in. I'm trying to convince them to get some chickens or ducks around here, but they think it'll put the guests off if they have to see where their eggs and meat come from."

I smirked. I bet they'd be less thrilled if they knew there had been a dead medic in the same room as the eggs and cheese.

"Do you want to see it?" he asked enthusiastically.

My mouth gaped open. "Sure," I said, taken aback. I almost tried to come up with an excuse to get out of it, but then I realized that I was about to reject an opportunity to learn more about Jamie and the rest of the resort.

He filled his glass and brought it along with him. I grabbed mine too, just to be a good sport. I was nervous as I watched him stumble down the sidewalk, but I figured he'd done this a thousand times before. Things must have been starting to liven up, because once the sun dipped below the still water, I heard voices emerge from the bars around the property.

We walked down the path a way before arriving at a metal-gated building. Jamie clumsily swung open the creaky gate and gestured inside. I pulled back the plastic curtain and was hit with a fresh wave of heat and humidity. It felt like being back in Miami.

Suddenly, overhead lights turned on, revealing rows and rows of greens. Jamie rejoined me and began to point out various plants.

"Here, we have your average herbs and spices. This is mint. We dry it out and use it in our tea. I think it's supposed to be good for digestion. I've got some lemongrass somewhere around here that's pretty good with it."

As we continued to walk, I could smell the booze seeping through Jamie's pores, yet he continued to take sips as he admired his plants. Every now and again, he would pause for a moment to spritz one with a water bottle.

"This is Thai ginger," he said, pointing to a pot. "That's a new one. That's spiral aloe, one of my favorites."

I vaguely remembered the names. Plants weren't really my thing. I didn't find it prudent to take notes, so

I just walked and allowed him to tell me about everything he grew.

"This is a special one," he said, his voice deepening as we approached a skinny tree with plain, flat leaves. It didn't look much different from any of the other trees. It bore small, circular fruit that did not look appetizing in the slightest. Looking down in the soil, I saw a plastic tag with a poison symbol on it.

"What is it?" I asked.

"It's a pong-pong tree. It's very rare and hard to get, though I managed to get one in here. The seeds are extremely toxic, so when I was purchasing the seeds, I had to provide proof that I had the means to nurture the plant and I wasn't going to eat the seeds to off myself." He giggled.

"Don't want anyone to mix that up with your tea garden," I said.

"I don't know how anyone could. I don't let a lot of people in here. There are only a couple of people I allow in here unsupervised. I don't want idiots coming in and ripping out all of my hard work. The plants I keep in here will one day go out there," he said, gesturing toward the outside resort. "Well, most of them will. This beauty will stay inside."

I heard the door open and the sound of feet pattering in our direction. I frowned when I saw two small children come running straight at us. For someone who said that he kept this place under wraps, he wasn't doing a very good job if children could get in.

"Jamie!" they cheered as they came to give him a hug. His drunken grin quickly changed to a sheepish expression as he set his glass of beer behind a potted fern. The kids began to chatter in a language I didn't know, though it sounded kind of like French. Jamie said a few words, though they were sluggish.

"Toby, Fantine, this is my friend, John," Jamie said, looking over at me. "He's visiting the island for a while. He's one of Max's friends from Florida."

"Hello," the kids said in unison, reaching out for my hands. I took their little hands in mine, giving them a small shake.

"Do you guys live here?" I asked, trying to place them into the greater scheme of things.

"Oh, yes," Toby said, his dark eyes big and round. "We help Jamie with his plants. We like it here."

Jamie smiled and patted the boy on his head. Toby turned his back to me and began speaking to Jamie directly.

"Today, we put the water on the lemon tree, just like you asked. And the pong-pong—"

"Thanks, guys," Jamie interrupted. "I think it's time for the two of you to go to bed. It's getting late."

"Goodnight," the kids said, giving Jamie a hug before running off.

Once they were gone, Jamie sighed and wiped the sweat from his forehead.

"I'm a terrible influence on them," he muttered, reaching for his beer.

"Who do they belong to?" I asked, still unsure as to why children were helping him in his greenhouse.

He shrugged. "That's the problem, isn't it? At this moment, they don't really belong to anyone."

"How so?" I asked, feeling mildly concerned that two unsupervised children were running loose at a very adult resort.

"A few years ago, I was visiting Haiti and met Toby and Fantine. If you can't tell, they're twins—ten years old now. They were orphans with no surviving family members to watch out for them. And they were indentured servants. Like, they were just little kids who were forced to do work just so they could have a roof over their heads and a little bit of food in their bellies."

"How did they get here? Did you adopt them?"

He shook his head and looked down at the floor. "No. I wish. I paid off their owner. They weren't happy there, and they were clearly malnourished. Even today, they're pretty small for their age."

"You bought them," I said, trying to clarify.

"I know it sounds terrible, but I didn't know what else to do. I put them on my private plane and brought them here, thinking I could work out their adoption while they lived in luxury for once. They live on-site and have a few nannies and tutors. They like to be in nature, so they come down here and work with me. I teach them all about the plants and they love it. They're so intelligent and have taken to a formal education so well."

I frowned. I couldn't fault him for wanting to give these kids a better life, but what he was doing didn't exactly seem legal. I didn't know their situation, but I didn't know if a court would find that it was best for the kids to be taken from their home.

"Why don't you just adopt them so they can be legal citizens and go to a regular school?" I asked, feeling curious.

He sighed. "My wife refuses. I've tried, but she has no connection to them. I already feel like a father to them. Those two mean the world to me and I want to raise them to be successful adults. I'd give them anything they could ever want, but they want so little. Actually, they just want a family to love them. It breaks my heart that I can't do that for them."

"Does your wife want biological children?" I questioned.

He scoffed. "I don't think so. I mean, it wouldn't be the end of the world if she did. She would probably enjoy sending them off to boarding school in designer clothes, then bragging to others about how well they're doing. The fact that the twins came from poverty in Haiti doesn't help."

I chuckled. "I would think that adopting a pair of orphans would give her some clout in society."

He shook his head. "Unfortunately, no. She's kind of old-school like that."

I nodded in understanding. She was probably a little racist and classist. I understood his code words.

I wanted to tell him to ditch the old woman if she was getting in the way of his deepest desires, but I had no room to talk. I had been in a failing relationship for a long time, and I'd only realized it when things got really bad.

"I'm worried she's never going to budge on this. I don't know what the kids are going to do when they get older. I used to talk to Dawn about this."

"And what did she say?"

He smiled. "She was great with those kids. She just told me to keep trying with Cara. Said she'd come around eventually. I think that was just wishful thinking."

"Were you close with Dawn?"

"Sometimes. I felt like she was just part of the family, in a way. I mean, not like a sister or anything." He giggled.

"Did you love her?"

He shook his head. "I love my wife. We just don't

always see eye to eye. Maybe I was too young when I got married. I was fresh out of college and Cara wanted a ring on her finger. If I wanted to keep her, I had to be a man."

I nodded. I had heard similar sentiments from former girlfriends.

"I think I need to go to bed," Jamie slurred, looking wobbly in his feet. We walked to the exit of the green-house together. I stood one step behind in case I needed to catch him.

"Are you okay walking back on your own?" I asked, thinking of all the bad things that could happen to a very drunk person at a resort. When I really thought about it, it was shocking that Dawn was their first fatality.

"Sure, sure," he said. "It was really nice to meet you. I know you're not here under the best circumstances, but I hope you can still enjoy your time here."

"Thanks," I said, shaking his massive hand. I waited a few beats as he walked toward his place. Then, I turned and walked in the opposite direction toward my room.

I could hear the party starting by the beach, yet my air-conditioned room called for me. My mouth was parched and I had only drunk a few beers. I couldn't imagine how bad Jamie was going to feel in the morning.

I couldn't help but feel very sorry for the Bergerons, Jamie, in particular. While he was rich and handsome, there was still a lot going on in his private life that the average spectator wouldn't know. While I may have suspected the brothers could have had something to do with Dawn's death upon first glance, I knew now that it wasn't very likely. Their grief felt genuine. I hadn't met with Sebastian yet, but I had a feeling he would also be devastated by the loss of his friend. Dawn seemed like a close companion to the three. I was beginning to wonder if there was anything to the rumor of their swapping partners, or if it was just legend stirred up in Max's wild imagination after a few too many drinks. After seeing how booze-addled the whole place was, I decided it was best to keep my wits about me, no matter how much I wanted to join in and feel numb to my personal problems that lay in the back of my mind.

CHAPTER EIGHT

W hen I awoke for breakfast the next morning, I found a note shoved under my door, requesting my presence at a staff meeting at ten o'clock in the office conference room. Already rising a little late, I jogged down to the buffet, grabbed a muffin and a banana, and jogged back to the office. I must have looked unprofessional as I found a seat in the back of the room, my face beet-red from exertion and the morning sun.

As I hastily ate my breakfast, I looked around the room at the staff. It couldn't have been a meeting of everyone involved in operations because I had just seen wait staff at the restaurant. I gathered that this meeting consisted of management and office positions. A hushed silence filled the room as Daniel took to the front to begin the meeting.

"Thank you all for working so hard amid an unspeakable tragedy," Daniel began. "I like to think of us as a family, and we have lost one of our own. At the moment, it is believed that Dawn succumbed to an undiagnosed heart condition and passed away in her room."

The room was dead silent. I tried to observe everyone there to see how people were reacting. For the most part, I only saw grief, perhaps fear. What I really wanted was to see smugness or guilt. If foul play was involved, someone had to know something.

"Now, I know that there are many rumors swirling around," Daniel continued. "I want to assure you all that you're perfectly safe here. But as a precaution, be careful of the substances you consume," he said. "It's no secret that our resort has come under scrutiny in the past for recreational drug and alcohol use. While our official stance is to ban all illegal substances, our protocol is loose out of trust for our guests. Our staff are our eyes and ears out there. Try to keep abreast on what the guests are doing. Instruct your staff to do the same. If you hear anything suspicious, please alert security or upper management. Come to us first instead of sharing your information with everyone around you."

I had the feeling that rumors had been an issue in the past, as Daniel seemed stern on this part. I had no problem listening to rumors. There was often a bit of truth in there, and not always in the way one might expect. A rumor could have not a shred of truth, but simply looking to the source of the lie could tell me everything I needed to know.

A hand went up in the room. Judging by his uniform, I guessed he was one of the restaurant or bar managers.

"When will we be informed of her actual cause of death?" he asked. "My sister said there was a newspaper article about Dawn's suspicious death. A heart defect doesn't seem very suspicious at all."

Daniel rubbed at his temple. "Yes, I'm sure many of you are aware that the press has gotten in on this. I have already released an official statement. We are working with law enforcement and detectives and are eager to find the truth. If you are approached by the press, I would implore you to decline any request for a statement. At the very least, just give your regrets to the family if you can't keep null on the matter. We don't need to make this harder than it already is. Too much negative press could harm our reservation numbers and our overall bottom line. That's not great when the quarterly bonuses are already being figured."

I raised my eyebrows in surprise. I understood why he wouldn't want rumors going straight to the press, but I though it was bold to so explicitly tell his staff to keep quiet. I wondered if he was trying to keep people from discovering something else.

"Now, on to our last point of business," he said. "You may have noticed that we have a newcomer in this meeting. I want to introduce you all to Mr. John Godwin. He's a former EMT from Miami, and he's here to fill the medic position until we have a permanent hire."

I furrowed my brow. I had not agreed to this. In fact, it had never been brought to my attention that there was any interest in my taking this position. I was so shocked that I couldn't do anything but sit in my seat, slack-jawed. The rest of the staff stared at me, some smiling, others blank-faced.

"I thought Max was filling in," a confused housekeeping manager asked. "That's what he told me when I talked to him last night." I stared at Daniel and wondered the same thing.

"Yes, but Max is not the right fit for the job," he said, lowering his voice. "Technically, he's a guest, so it doesn't make sense to have him working as an employee. We appreciate his help, but it's better to hire someone fresh."

"It's a liability," Sebastian jumped in, looking bored. "If a minor ailment is mistreated because our medic is wasted, we're going down. We've got insurance and waivers for your average accidents, but not for serious ignorance and carelessness. We need someone competent to take care of any illness or injury, especially with a storm coming."

"A storm?" I asked. No one had said anything about a storm. The rest of the meeting attendants seemed to know more about this than I did.

Daniel frowned. "I figured Max would have mentioned it when he picked you up. The weather on the island can be a bit unpredictable, but we have reports from the Coast Guard telling us that we're due to have a minor storm in a few days."

"Like a hurricane?" I asked, feeling concerned. I had been through a few hurricanes in my day, and I had seen how destructive they could be miles inland. I had never experienced one on an island. I know Max said they weren't so bad, but I had to wonder if he was a little oblivious to just how bad things could get.

He shook his head. "Not that severe. We probably won't have as many guests here when it hits, but there will be some. And they will be perfectly safe. This place is designed to withstand anything nature throws at us. But that means that our restaurant and bar managers need to ensure that no urgent deliveries are supposed to go out at that time. If there's something we can't live without, get it now."

I sighed. Even if I managed to solve this thing by the next day, I still wouldn't be able to leave. Not only did I have an extra job I'd never asked for, but I would be trapped here when the storm blew through. I wasn't keen on staying here for long, but I really didn't want to brave a boat ride in choppy water.

"Well, that's all I've got," Daniel said. "Thank you all for your continued cooperation."

I sat in my seat and waited as the rest of the staff filed out. People muttered quietly among each other, mostly rumblings about having to work during a storm. I heard someone mention something about power outages. Once everyone was gone, I stormed up to the front of the room, looking for answers.

"I'm the medic?" I asked Daniel. "I was brought here as a private investigator. I haven't worked as a medic in years. How can you give me a job without asking me first?"

Daniel sighed. "Look, it's clear that you're not a guest. You don't party, you lurk around and observe people, and you spend too much time with Max. The staff was about to get suspicious. If they see a private investigator, they will think something is wrong. And if they happen to know something—"

"They wouldn't tell me," I finished.

"Exactly. Besides, Max is a good guy, but he really is a liability as a medic. With the storm coming, we won't be able to send any cases to the mainland. We need someone competent here in case of emergency."

I chewed my lip. It seemed as though Daniel had thought this over rather thoroughly. I understood where he was coming from and his plan made perfect sense, but I still would have liked to be involved in the decision making.

"This wasn't what I signed up for," I said. "What if I'm too busy working a fake job to do any research?"

Daniel shook his head. "It shouldn't be a problem. For the most part, your job will be an on-call basis. You can hang out in the doctor's office, but you don't have to stay there. Besides, people tend to trust medical professionals. You might get the right person talking."

He did have a point. If I could get the right people to open up to me, I might be able to figure out whether Dawn died of anything besides a simple heart attack. I wasn't thrilled to get back into medicine, but it was something I was capable of.

"We're going to compensate you, of course," Sebastian added. "While we appreciate Max's offer to provide your services, we're going to make sure you're well taken care of while you investigate. Plus, you'll be paid for your work as the resort medic."

"We're prepared to help you out in any way we can," Daniel said, speaking in code again. "It goes without saying that you can stay here for free whenever you want."

I nodded. "Fine. I'll be the medic. But I can't stick around here forever."

"Of course," Daniel said. "We know that we're taking you from your life on the mainland. We wouldn't ask this of you if it weren't important."

I gritted my teeth. They had no idea that I truly didn't have anything going for me back at home. The thought of my newly-acquired loneliness made my stomach sink.

With the prospect of being paid handsomely dangling over my head, it was hard to get too upset about this new surprise. When I finally returned, I would have to drop a lot of money to get a new place. At least at the resort, I could have somewhere to live for free. Plus, if I wasn't completely sick of this place by the time the job was done, maybe I'd bide my time here until I knew what my next move would be. It was hard to say no to free rent and meals. I didn't love the beach, but I could always hang out in my room and order room service.

"So, what's going to happen to Max? Does he know that's he's not the medic anymore?"

Sebastian smiled. "I notified him this morning. I think he celebrated the news with a drink."

I scoffed. "Have you guys ever thought about opening a luxury rehab facility? You could refer just about every one of your guests."

Sebastian and Jamie chuckled while Daniel pursed his lips.

"Maybe when this is through, we can hire you on to develop some of these ideas," Sebastian joked.

Daniel didn't seem amused by the lightheartedness. He looked like he hadn't slept in days. I figured his brothers were allowed to deal with the tragedy while he'd had to put his grieving on hold to attend to the resort.

I was a little surprised to see that the brothers generally seemed glad to have me around. I had learned that the presence of a private investigator was not always a welcome sight. However, all three men had been very cooperative so far. I had wondered if jealousy between the brothers could have spurred a violent reaction toward their rumored lover, but they seemed to get along well with each other and with me. The more time I spent around them, the more I disliked them as suspects. They seemed to be pretty clean in regard to the death. Their private lives were a different story.

CHAPTER NINE

Upon starting my first shift as resort medic, I realized that Daniel had downplayed the role. By the time I got to the tiny medical clinic, I had a patient. A drowsy college student begged me to give him an IV for his wicked hangover that he assured me would kill him. I figured that IV fluids seemed extreme, so I handed him an electrolyte drink to sip while checking his vitals. When he checked out, medically speaking, I handed him a bottle of water and some anti-nausea medication and sent him to his room to rest, with orders to keep the boozing to a minimum for at least a day.

Next, I had a few embarrassed young women ask me if we carried emergency contraception. I thought it was an odd request until I opened the store cupboard and saw boxes upon boxes of Plan B lined up on the shelf. I handed boxes out like it was Halloween. I asked no questions and received no tales. Eventually, I began handing out condoms as well, then charged the medication to the patients' rooms. Easy.

I was starting to feel a little like a school nurse. I handed out bandages to people with blistered heels, antacids to those who overindulged in food and drink, and I applied cool compresses to horrific sunburns. People seemed very appreciative of my services, and I did so very little. I was starting to see how it could be a very appealing job to a young medical professional, or a retired one, at that. I wasn't exactly sure how much I was getting paid, but I didn't really care.

Then, I had to go on a few house calls. The first one was to the kitchen where a cook got distracted and sliced into her finger. I grabbed my kit and met the woman in a small office. She was clutching a dishtowel to her finger, looking nervous.

I peeked at it and decided that it wasn't deep enough to require stitches. After sanitizing the wound, I used a special glue that doctors liked to use on minor cuts. As I applied the glue, we chatted about the menu they were working on. Apparently, supper was supposed to be especially good, and she encouraged me to enjoy my dinner in the dining room. Once the cut was closed, I wrapped it in gauze and tape and sent her on her way.

Later, I had to go to the bar to deal with a mild case of alcohol poisoning. I noticed that the bartender had been arguing with the security guard, who was trying to drag the ill man away from the crowd of tourists.

"What's going on?" I asked the guard.

"Over serving," he grunted, scowling at the bartender. "They can hand out as many drinks as they want, but we have to deal with the aftermath."

"It's kind of hard to count when they're getting drinks from all over the place," the bartender argued. "I'm doing my best."

"Not good enough," the guard said under his breath.

I bent down and felt the guy's pulse. It was a little slow but still within a normal range. He was out cold, but as long as there was nothing else going on with him, I was pretty sure he would be better with time.

"Want me to call a cart to send him to your office?" the guard asked.

"Let's do that," I replied. "I'll give him an IV and let him sleep it off. He should probably be monitored."

As we waited for backup to arrive, I began to talk to the guard a little more.

"Does this kind of thing happen often?" I asked.

"At least once a week," the guard muttered. "I get that people like to have fun, but this seems a little outrageous."

"The same with drugs?" I asked.

"Yeah, about. I don't know if you know this, but you've got activated charcoal and a variety of overdose antidotes up there."

"Thanks," I replied. "I'm still getting to know my lay of the land."

"No problem. Here's your cart," he said, pointing to the gator cruising in our direction.

"Say, before I go, I have a question for you," I asked nervously. "Do you think Dawn really died of a heart attack?"

He snorted. "Are you worried that something's going to happen to you now that you're the medic? I wouldn't worry about that."

"So you think someone gave her something?"

"I guess we'll find out when the coroner gives their final report. The least Daniel could do is tell us truthfully what happened to her. I'm worried it's just going to be swept under the rug."

"Why do you say that?" I asked as we loaded the guy onto the stretcher and fastened the straps.

The guard shook his head. "No reason, really. No one really thinks of the little people when the power players have problems."

"You don't care for Daniel?"

"That's not what I'm saying. He's a good guy, but he's a control freak. If something bad happened, I don't think he would want anyone to know. That's all. I've got to get back to my post. Do you need anything else?"

"No," I said as I hastily got in the passenger's seat. "You've been very helpful. Thank you."

"No problem," he said, waving as we rushed back to my office. I thought about what he said as I hooked up an IV and waited for the drunk guy to wake up. Daniel did seem to be pretty good at keeping up appearances. He wasn't unfriendly, but he was rather rigid. Looking back at his talk about the staff being one big family, it kind of came off as disingenuous. He was a businessman trying to keep his resort afloat. I still wanted to ask him more questions, but I would have to be careful not to trust him implicitly. He had a lot to lose if the investigation showed something that didn't suit him. Perhaps I was hired to ensure everything was fine, but I could also be used as a first defense in protecting his good name. If I reported directly to him about any strange findings, he would have time to get out in front of the hypothetical shit storm.

Eventually, the drunk guy woke up and was utterly confused. I nearly had to hold him down to keep him from ripping the IV out of his arm. Finally, he managed to settle down and let the rest of the fluids drip into his system. I gave him a ginger ale and lectured him on binge-drinking for the rest of his stay before entering a hefty fee into the billing system. Then, when he was well enough to leave on his own accord, I sent him on his way.

Meanwhile, my phone had found service and a flood of texts and calls came in from across the sea. I didn't bother answering, but I read all the messages Marcie typed out. At first, they were very apologetic. Then, once she realized that I had left her high and dry, they got nasty. She told me that I was the one at fault for her infidelities because I wasn't a good enough lover. She then recalled every way I had wronged her in the past three years and reminded me of how shitty I was.

I couldn't lie—it hurt to see her write such terrible things about me. We had been close. Admittedly, our relationship had become somewhat stagnant in recent years, mostly due to the fact that we were reaching the end of our prime and were comfortable with where we were.

I wanted to respond with a rebuttal and defend myself in some way, but it was useless. Perhaps it had been petty to cut off all means of survival. However, it wasn't as though she was alone in the world. I wasn't that cruel. Yes, she would be uncomfortable for quite some time. If she never found another man to take care of her, she would likely be uncomfortable forever. But after what she did to me, it seemed like justice.

It would be hard to go to bed every night without

her. I didn't have someone I could call or text at a moment's notice to talk about my day. I'd be eating dinners for one for the foreseeable future. I would also likely be celibate for some time to come. I was sad—I couldn't deny that. As tough as I wanted to feel after kicking her out of my place without any backup plans, I still felt weak and vulnerable. Perhaps I wasn't the best boyfriend, but I didn't deserve to have my heart broken in such a brazen fashion.

I heard the door to my office start to open, so I silenced my phone and stashed it in a desk drawer. I figured I'd be introducing myself to a tourist with heat exhaustion, but instead, I saw the skinny blonde from the previous night glaring at me.

"Hi, I'm John," I said extending my hand to her.

"I know," she replied, rejecting my handshake. She folded her arms across her torso.

"You must be Cara Bergeron," I said, my last image of her being railed by her brother-in-law.

"I want to know who the fuck you think you are," she hissed.

I blinked. "I'm John. I'm the substitute medic."

"You're a private investigator," she snarled. "Jamie told me all about you."

"Yeah?" I asked. I couldn't imagine he'd said anything bad about me. I thought he seemed to like me when he was leading the tour of the greenhouse.

"I know that you're here because that woman died. What did the coroner tell you?" She leaned toward me, as if she were a cobra ready to strike.

"She said that it was cardiac arrest."

"Caused by?"

I blinked. "Perhaps a congenital heart defect. It's not certain at this moment."

"So then it's settled. Why are you still here?"

I frowned. "I don't see the harm in being thorough. If something dangerous were happening, wouldn't you want to know? I mean, hypothetically, your life could be in danger."

"Is that a threat?" she hissed.

"What? No, it's not a threat," I said exasperatedly. Max had not exaggerated when he described this woman. She was a nightmare.

"What's your game?" she sneered.

"Game?" I asked innocently. "I truly have no idea what you're talking about."

"Cara," a booming voice said from the hallway. Daniel entered my office, fury in his eyes.

"What?" she asked.

"Why are you bothering John? I hired him. I want him to be here. I don't want the whole resort knowing that we have some extra security measures. It makes people nervous."

"We don't even know who he is. He could be a spy,

sent from a competitor, or a rapist looking for a quiet place to commit a crime."

"Hey," Daniel and I said in unison.

"Max recommended him," Daniel said.

"That old creep? I don't trust him. Have you seen the way he looks at me like I'm a piece of meat?"

I rolled my eyes. "Doubt it," I muttered under my breath.

"Cara, chill the fuck out," Daniel said. I was surprised by this. I hadn't seen any personality come out of that man. He had a fire in his eyes that I found slightly frightening.

"Don't talk to me like that," she spat.

"Cara, no one likes a drunk bitch," he said. I raised my eyebrows in shock.

Her entire face changed. It went from smugness to absolute hatred. I thought she was going to explode with rage.

"Oh, is this sexual frustration?" she screeched. "You want to fuck me so bad, but you couldn't get it up if you tried."

I took a step back. I realized that I was no longer part of the conversation. I wanted to leave the room, but they were standing in front of the only exit.

"What the fuck are you talking about?"

"Your impotence," she sneered.

"My what? You've lost your damn mind. I think

you need to eat. It's been a few days. Maybe take a nap. Did you only get nine hours of sleep last night?"

"You're a little bitch."

"You're a toxic whore," Daniel said, causing Cara to storm off.

"I'm very sorry you had to see that," Daniel said, sinking down into a chair. "It's something that shouldn't go beyond the family home. I try so damn hard to get along with her for my brother's sake. She really is a toxic whore, though."

I chuckled. "I used to be with a toxic whore," I said. "In fact, I caught her cheating the day before I came here."

"That's awful."

"I know. I came here as a way to run away from my problems, I suppose."

"Nothing wrong with that. I think that's the reason I stayed single. It's easier that way."

"I get it. I'm sure it's not easy to foster relationships when you're constantly surrounded by short flings."

He nodded. "And work gets in the way. I don't think I'm missing out on anything, especially after seeing what Jamie's gone though. He loves her and I don't know why."

"Maybe she has some redeeming qualities," I said, trying to play devil's advocate.

He scoffed. "Maybe she's weird in bed. I wouldn't

know. Crazy can be good, but she's too crazy for me. Anyway, I'm sorry that you had to see all of that. If you don't mind, would you consider keeping it to yourself? I don't want our staff to think they're being led by a couple of psychos. I assure you, I'm really not like this."

"Got it," I said, having no use in spreading information. I could just take down all the information in my notebook.

"Thanks. I'll see you later. Why don't you sit with us at dinner tonight? It's Cajun night—a new menu and everything. We'd like to have you with us."

"Sounds great," I said, giving a fake smile. "I'll see you then."

Once he was gone, I started laughing uncontrollably. I was so shocked at what I had just seen that I didn't even know how to respond. I thought my situation with Marcie was bad, but Daniel seemed to have it worse and he had nothing to do with that relationship. I guess I had nothing to do but sit and count my blessings that my toxic whore was out of the picture.

CHAPTER TEN

T hough I felt uncomfortable sitting in the dining room with the Bergeron family, I accepted Daniel's offer but chose to sit at a separate table with Max. After the spat with Cara, I didn't want to do anything to provoke her further. She looked sullen sitting between Jamie and Sebastian, poking around her salad. Mostly, she clutched a martini and shot glances at me from a few yards away.

Daniel was his normal, stony self. He sat on the opposite side of the table from his sister-in-law, gritting his teeth every time she spoke. I couldn't imagine having to take part in that family dynamic on a daily basis. It was surprising that the brothers were so close, despite her. If she wasn't yelling at one, she was screwing the other, and her poor husband was out of the loop.

Eventually, I would need to find time to talk to Sebastian. He was louder and more outgoing than the other two, but perhaps not as friendly. It wasn't as though he wasn't nice, but his bold personality made it easy for me to write him off as an asshole. Still, he was another important piece of the puzzle, and eventually, I would have to get a good feel for who he was as a person. I already knew he had a warped sense of family loyalty, as he had no problem helping Cara cheat on Jamie. If that was any indication of his overall character, I wouldn't be surprised if I found more dirt on him.

Naturally, Max wanted to know every detail of my day, though I had told Daniel I would be discreet.

"Mix in a water and I'll tell you what I know," I said as the waiter came around to refill glasses.

He listened, sucking back a few gulps of ice water.

"Max, do you ever get tired of entertaining yourself with other people's drama?" I asked exasperatedly.

"No, not at all," he said earnestly. "I don't have a lot going on in my life. I'm in my fifties, widowed, retired, and my kids are all grown up. I've always been interested in how things work. It's what led me to go to medical school. Then, when I decided that I really didn't care about medicine, it was too late. I had to make money somehow, so I taught and worked long hours. When my wife died, I was financially comfortable. When her life insurance check came in, I didn't know what to do with it. But she always told me that she wanted me to be happy, no matter what."

"So you quit your job," I concluded.

"It's more than that. I started observing people. I watched and figured out what made them tick. I listened to their stories. Then, when I'm feeling inspired, I write my own, using the tiny bits of knowledge I've collected over the years. One day, I'd like to sell those books and let other people in on the knowledge I've collected."

I raised my eyebrows. "You make snooping sound so impressive and artistic."

He laughed. "And you've made it a career. Now, tell me about your first day on the job."

I recounted the various injuries and ailments as if I were a resident reporting to my attending. He listened patiently and nodded as I rattled off my list.

"Par for the course," he concluded. "It sounds like you're doing a good job."

This meant a lot, even now. Max hadn't been my instructor for many years, but I thought very highly of his opinion.

"So," he continued. "What have you learned about the case?"

I didn't want to give too much away. I trusted Max, but I didn't think it would be very professional to gossip about a very serious manner. After all, I had been hired to be discreet. So, I tried not to tell him much more than he already knew.

"The Bergerons are a strange family," I said. "Have you ever seen the brothers fight?"

He thought for a moment. "Not anything significant. If they do, they keep it under wraps. Daniel isn't the type to air his dirty laundry. Sebastian doesn't really give a shit about anything—he's too laid back. I've seen Jamie get angry before, but for the most part, he's in control of his emotions."

"When have you seen him angry?"

He tapped his water glass with his fingernail as he thought. "Oh, I've seen him get pissed off at guests before. One night, a young couple thought it would be cute to have sex inside his greenhouse. He caught them disobeying the *Keep Out* signs and nearly lost his shit. If Dawn hadn't been there to calm him down, he would have hit someone."

"Dawn was with him?"

He shrugged. "Like I said, they were pals. For the most part, you're not going to see a Bergeron and a laborer hang out together. People around here tend to hang out with people of their own ranking. So, on days off, the housekeeping staff will have daiquiris at the pool, or the managers will play cards on the private employee deck. In terms of the unofficial hierarchy, she was near the top, so it was perfectly normal for her to hang out with any of the brothers."

"Hypothetically, if she had been given something to make her sick, it wouldn't be by a busboy then, right?"

Max mused for a while. "That would make sense. You're right. She would have spent more time with the upper echelon."

"And where's the line between upper and lower employees?"

"Oh, probably anyone who would attend one of their staff meetings."

My eyes lit up. If one of her coworkers had given her something to cause her death, they would have been with me in that meeting. That narrowed the suspect list by about seventy-five percent.

"But she didn't just hang out with co-workers," Max added. "If there was a good party going on, it wouldn't be unlike her to join in. She liked to mingle with guests on occasion."

I dropped my head. We were back to square one.

I watched as Sebastian got up from his table and walked over to us. He stuck out his hand in front of me, his bright smile dazzling in my face.

"I was told I should introduce myself," he said warmly. "We haven't officially met yet."

"It's nice to meet you," I said. "You're the only Bergeron I haven't spoken to."

"Saving the best for last," he joked. "I've been busy the past few days with everything going on, but I wouldn't mind having a drink sometime."

I nearly laughed in his face. He certainly had been busy, at least the previous night. "Yeah, that would be cool," I said casually.

"Great," he said. "I don't know if I'll be able to help you solve this thing, but I'll try to help in any way I can."

"That means a lot," I said, extending my hand for a handshake.

Sebastian patted me on the back and returned to his table. Max stifled a laugh.

"What?" I asked.

"Nothing. He seems particularly chipper tonight. He must know he's getting some ass."

I carefully glanced at the family table and watched the brothers talk. Sebastian was laughing and occasionally elbowing Cara in the arm. She didn't seem particularly amused and continued to sip her martini through tight lips.

Finally, the main course arrived. A plate of steaming-hot jambalaya was placed in front of me by a friendly waiter. Max licked his lips and dug in. I took a few bites, my mouth already on fire.

"Did you get the right plates?" I heard Cara ask the waiter, her voice sharp.

"What are you talking about?" Jamie asked.

"I'm not eating white rice," she said stuffily. "I asked the kitchen for some modifications."

"Yes, ma'am. We have prepared yours with quinoa," the waiter said nervously.

"Good," she said as the plate was set down in front of her. Even with the modifications to her meal, she didn't touch her food.

"Does she always do that?" I asked quietly. "The kitchen staff must hate her. They would have had to make a completely separate batch for her. Who orders jambalaya without the rice?"

Max shook his head. "I told you she was difficult. I wouldn't be surprised if she sent it back and asked for something completely different."

"What does Jamie see in her?" I asked, though mostly to myself.

"Not a damn clue," Max said, resuming his boozing. "If we were the last two people on Earth, I still wouldn't touch her with a ten-foot pole."

My dinner was interrupted by a sweaty chef ambushing my table. I had hardly taken more than three bites before being called into work.

"We have a guest with an allergic reaction," he panted. "It must be the shellfish."

I sighed and tossed my napkin onto the chair. "There are crawfish on the side of the plate. Wouldn't you know better if you were allergic to shellfish?"

"Don't give these people too much credit," Max said. "Do you want my help?"

"Can you run to the office and grab a few supplies?" I asked. "I should make sure he's stable."

We parted ways as Max waddled to the medical office and I followed the chef to the sick diner. I found the guy wheezing in his seat as the other diners swarmed around him.

"Back up, please," I said as I made my way through the crowd.

I knelt beside the young man and listened to his breathing. His face was becoming puffy and splotchy, but he still had a clear airway.

"Do you have any known allergies?" I asked, though I already suspected the answer.

"Shellfish," he squeaked.

"Do you have medication with you?" I asked.

He shook his head in response.

"Well, I have someone going to my office to get some for you. Until then, I want you to continue taking smooth, even breaths, okay? Can you do that for me?"

He nodded and closed his eyes for a moment, concentrating on his breathing. As I listened to his breathing, I heard it become more strained and ragged.

I really didn't want to have to call a helicopter if I didn't absolutely have to. A minute later, Max came zipping down with my pouch of miscellaneous medical supplies.

I wasn't sure how bad this guy's allergy was, so I used the EpiPen, just to be safe. Within minutes, his breathing returned to normal and his face looked a little less splotchy. His dining companions returned to their seats, looking relieved.

"Now, I'm going to advise that you take an antihistamine, grab a sandwich from the buffet, and eat somewhere else," I said. "If you have any other symptoms, make sure to see me. And please do your best to stay away from the shellfish for the rest of your stay. Your waiters will give you a list of ingredients if you ask."

The guy nodded sheepishly. Once I decided he would be okay, I packed up my bag and returned with Max to our dining room. My stomach was rumbling and I was sure our food was now cold.

When we returned, the Bergerons and their tablemates were finishing supper, except for Sebastian and Cara, who had left in the time it took us to stabilize our patient. I looked over at Max and he immediately cracked a smile.

"Oh, I wonder where they went," he said innocently.

I couldn't help but laugh too. I liked Jamie, but if

he didn't know what was going on behind his back, he must be an idiot.

"Sebastian is a shady guy," Max said, returning to his meal. "When he came over here to introduce himself, he was laying on the charm pretty thickly," he said emphatically.

"Shady enough to harm the medic?" I asked.

Max inhaled sharply. "Don't ask me. But if I had to bet on any of the Bergerons to get caught up in something bad, it would be Sebastian. Again, I'm not saying he would, just that if anyone were to, it would surprise me the least if his name came up."

I nodded. "That's good to know. I'll have to be on guard when I interview him. Think he'll follow through with his offer for drinks?"

Max shrugged. "I guess we'll see."

Max and I finished our dinner alone as the sun dipped below the horizon. After a long day of work that I never asked for, I was ready for a shower and a bed. Unfortunately, my work was never-ending. As I got up from my seat and rubbed my full stomach, my pager began to beep.

"Let me come with you," Max requested. "I hate the responsibility, but I get bored."

"Whatever." I groaned as we walked up the incline toward the medical office. I had no idea how Dawn ever had time to party. I had been on the job for one day and I was already thinking about asking Daniel for a raise. I hardly had the time to eat, much less time to take drugs. Perhaps no one considered how the job affected a person. As I climbed toward the office for the third or fourth time that day, I started to understand how one could have a heart attack from this lifestyle. Perhaps it just took a new perspective to see that.

CHAPTER ELEVEN

Expecting another case of alcohol overdose or even another shellfish allergy, I had already mentally checked out of my medical duties. However, the screaming that I heard as I approached the office caused my heart to race.

"He's dying!" a female voice shrieked. Nothing could have prepared me to spot Cara's tear-soaked face peeking out from my office, begging for help.

"What's going on?" I asked.

"There's something wrong with Sebastian," she said. "He needs to go to the mainland, immediately."

Sebastian was on the examination table, his eyes rolling back into his head. He was drifting in and out of consciousness and was certainly in no condition to tell me what was wrong with him.

"Does he suffer from any known illnesses or conditions?" I asked Cara.

"No—I don't think so. Listen to me. Call a helicopter."

I could see he was very ill, but I didn't know enough to make that call just yet. As I'd discovered with the man suffering from an allergic reaction, I could handle a serious medical condition on my own.

"I need to check—"

"Call the fucking helicopter!" she screamed.

I looked at Max, who quickly scurried to the phone. I could hear him speaking with someone in hushed tones, completely unlike him. That's when I realized I was dealing with something beyond my pay grade. Max returned to my side just in time to roll Sebastian over onto his side as he began to vomit.

Cara stood in the corner, shaking. Her face was now pale enough to match her platinum hair.

"What happened?" I asked again in a calm but firm voice. "If we're going to help him, I need to know as much as possible. How did he get like this?"

She shook her head violently. "I don't know. We were at dinner, then he said he wasn't feeling well. I wasn't hungry so I volunteered to walk with him to get some antacids or something from the medical office. He said his stomach hurt and he started to throw up. I wondered if he had gotten food poisoning from our meal. I wasn't sick, but I didn't eat the shrimp. I thought that you'd have some medicine to make him feel better. I gave him some of this," she said, pointing to a very old bottle of Ipecac syrup.

"No one even uses that anymore," I muttered to myself. "You thought he had food poisoning or heartburn and you tried to make him throw up more? You can't give someone too much of that. How much did he have?"

She shrugged. "Not much," she said frantically. "He couldn't get it down."

I sighed. "No shit," I whispered under my breath. "Can you tell me if he was using any drugs or drinking heavily? He didn't seem drunk when I talked to him, but did he do any shots or something after I left?"

She shook her head again. "Nothing like that—at least, I don't think so. I would have no way to know."

I checked Sebastian's vitals and easily concluded that he was in danger. His heart rate was through the roof and his pupils weren't dilating. I wasn't sure if it was the spice from the food or blood in his vomit, but I guessed it could very well be both. As I examined him, he was hardly conscious.

"How long does it usually take for a helicopter to get here?" I asked Max.

"I'm not sure. I assume you'll have one within twenty minutes or so."

I shook my head. "That's too long. What do you think we should do until then?"

Max shrugged. He was just as stumped as I was. "Perhaps give him a saline solution. I don't think we can give him anything else until we know what's wrong with him."

I set up an IV line as Max rummaged through the cupboard full of drugs. He filled a syringe and injected it into my line.

"Beta blockers," he said. "It might get his heart rate under control."

I grabbed a stethoscope and listened to his heart again. His heart rate was still high, but not near as high as it had been. Unfortunately, he was slipping into unconsciousness as we spoke.

"It could be an overdose of amphetamines," I suggested to Max. "That would explain the increased heart rate."

I grabbed a lancet and poked a small hole in Sebastian's finger. I put the droplet of blood into a solution, then dipped a drug test strip in it. The strip remained unchanged.

"If it is, this test didn't pick up on it," I said, feeling more confused.

By now, Cara was rocking back and forth on the balls of her feet. She looked like she was going to faint.

"Do you need to sit down?" I asked.

She shook her head and continued sniffling.

"Can you have someone track Jamie down?" I asked Max. "She shouldn't be here right now—not alone, anyway."

Max grimaced. "I don't want anyone to see him like this in case he doesn't make it. Then again, the family should know what's going on. I'll call security and have someone bring the brothers up here."

I heard him go to the phone and politely request that someone send the other Bergerons up to the medical office. His voice was calm, but I could still hear the urgency in his voice.

Sebastian was looking worse by the minute, but there was nothing more we could do. Cara remained tight-lipped in the corner, not giving us any information that would help us diagnose her brother-in-law.

After what felt like hours, the helicopter arrived. Paramedics rushed in with a stretcher and collected Sebastian. I felt helpless as they asked me questions about his condition and I was unable to provide any useful information.

"He was complaining of stomach pains, vomited, then collapsed," I said. "She said he thought he had indigestion or food poisoning, but it's obvious that's not the case. As far as we know, he didn't ingest any drugs. I really wish I could tell you more, but I can't. We gave him saline and beta blockers, but he's only gotten worse since he's been up here."

"Well, we'll take him back to Miami," the medic said.

I quickly scribbled down my phone number and handed it to the medic. "Give this to the doctors. Tell them to contact me with his status," I said softly, pressing the paper into his hand.

"Got it," he replied shortly, tucking it into his uniform pocket. As they were carting him back to the helicopter landing pad, Daniel and Jamie came jogging to the office.

"What's wrong with him?" Jamie asked.

I shook my head. "We don't know. He's being taken to Miami. We did as much as we could, but it's really not apparent what's wrong with him other than that he's really sick."

Jamie put his arm around his wife. "Were you with him when he got sick? He was fine just an hour ago."

She shook her head and looked like she was about to be sick herself. "I have no idea what happened," she said mournfully. "I was only walking with him when he started feeling bad. I wish I could tell you more, but I can't."

"It's okay," Jamie said softly, pulling his wife's head into his muscular chest. "You did the right thing by bringing him up here. He'll be okay."

I bit my lip. I had seen doctors do amazing things, but I wasn't expecting Sebastian to make a quick recovery.

Daniel ran a hand through his slicked-back hair. He kept looking over at Cara and glaring. I found it curious.

"Does anyone here know if he might have taken anything?" I asked gingerly. "If we have a few good guesses, I can call the hospital and give them a heads-up. It could make a huge difference."

Jamie shrugged. "I don't know. He had a few drinks at dinner, but he usually does. Otherwise, he seemed sober."

Daniel grimaced. "Would male supplements have this sort of effect on someone?"

I looked at Max for backup.

He bit his lip. "It shouldn't—not like that, anyway. Do you know what exactly he was using?"

"Oh, I don't," Daniel replied. "It was merely conjecture," he said, glancing at Cara. It seemed as though Daniel was in on the family secret.

"I want to lie down," Cara whined.

Jamie nodded. "I'll take you home," he said, his big blue eyes full of worry.

Daniel put his hands on his hips. "I'm going to call my parents."

"Hey, Daniel," I said before he walked out of my

office. He turned around and gave me a curious look. "About what you said about male enhancement—" I said awkwardly.

"It was nothing," he interrupted. "I don't know why I said it. Actually, I do know why I said it. Sebastian and Cara are always running off together, giving the stupidest excuses. I'm certain that Jamie knows and is just trying to deal with it on his own. It's just hard to watch, you know? I love Sebastian, but he can be so selfish sometimes. I'm sorry I had to bring my family problems into something serious."

"It's fine," I said. "It was shocking for everyone. I'm hoping he'll pull through. He should be in good hands."

Daniel nodded wordlessly and left the office. I waited a full minute before turning to Max.

"As far as we know, Sebastian is a perfectly healthy man. Without warning, he keels over and falls unconscious. As far as we know, he hasn't taken any intoxicants. It can't be food poisoning, because everyone else ate the same thing and is fine. Besides, it wouldn't come on that quickly."

"Just like Dawn," Max said. "They were both fine before they weren't."

I nodded. "Precisely. Do you think Daniel was serious when he talked about sexual enhancements, or was he just taking a dig at Cara?"

Max shrugged. "I'm not sure. However, I don't think one of those pills could do that much damage. Besides, those are usually for men."

I shook my head. "Hear me out on this—what if they were both taking something to boost libido or function? It seems like it's common knowledge that the two of them had strong sexual appetites. Would it be so crazy if they were taking the same thing and someone had spiked it with something else? Or, maybe it was poisoned. Neither were reported to be high, so we just assumed they were clean."

Max raised his eyebrows. "That would be pretty serious. I don't know how you're going to find out whether they were taking such a substance if neither of them is able to tell us. I guess you could always ask for permission to search his room."

I scoffed. "That will go over well with Cara. She seems to think I'm up to something."

"She's out of her damned mind. You'd have to be an idiot to get in the way of the one person who could figure this thing out."

"Would it make any sense that both of them were poisoned?" I asked, struggling to find a cause for two mysterious cases of serious illness.

"I'd say it seems a lot more likely now that it's happened twice. What kind of poisoning were you thinking?"

"That's where I keep getting stuck. I have no idea how the poison would be introduced. But it's got to be something that wouldn't come up on your average toxicology screening. Something like oleander poisoning, perhaps."

"What's that?"

"It's a toxic plant. I vaguely remember reading about it once. I guess it's something one might use to discreetly murder someone."

"Huh," Max said, obviously unconvinced but trying to appear supportive.

"I think I'm going to go down to the greenhouse and take a look around," I said as I got up from my seat. Max started to follow me.

"Are you coming with me?" I asked.

"No," he said, his voice low and gruff. "I could use a drink or two."

I opened my mouth to scold him, but I decided against it. I think he was right about that.

After searching around for a light switch, I began my search of the building. I looked up a picture of oleander and tried to match the photograph to the various plants growing onsite. Luckily, Jamie had marked all plants with their common name and scientific name. It took me nearly an hour of checking and double-checking before realizing I had hit a dead end with this hunch. There wasn't a single oleander plant in the greenhouse. And I figured that meant there were none on the grounds, since Jamie liked to landscape with his own work. Feeling mentally exhausted and bummed out by the night's events, I headed to Max's favorite bar to have just one drink.

"Any luck?" he asked as the bartender slid a beer in my direction.

I shook my head. "No oleander. It was a pretty wild long shot, wasn't it?"

"You never know," he said, taking a swig. "It's just too bad we didn't figure out what it was so we could tell the doctors working on him. But whatever they find should help you figure out what killed Dawn. Plus, you'll know how to treat it immediately if it happens again."

"True," I said, feeling hopeful and thankful that we caught it early in Sebastian.

I began to unwind a little as I drank—so much so that I ordered a second beer and a plate of nachos to share with Max. Since my dinner was interrupted, I didn't realize how hungry I was. For the first time since I'd arrived, I was starting to loosen up and relax.

This feeling of lightness came to an end when a security guard passed me a note as I was preparing to order a third drink. I unfolded it and held it up so Max could read it too.

MY BROTHER PASSED AWAY this evening around eleven. As of now, the doctors have no idea what happened to him. Their best guess is that he suffered from some sort of heart-related episode. I've requested that a full autopsy and a thorough toxicology report be conducted. We could have some news by as soon as next week. I understand that you have a job to do, and by all means, do it. I just thought you should be aware that my brother and I are in grieving and will likely stay away from resort operations as much as possible. It's just too painful to walk among cheery people right now. If you need anything for your day-to-day work, I encourage you to speak with someone in the front office. They will be happy to help.

Also, I want to thank you and Max for your efforts in saving my brother. I know you tried very hard to revive him, but the doctors assured me that not much could be done in his advanced illness. We are lucky to have such a talented and compassionate medic in our resort.

-Daniel

I CRUMPLED up the letter and stuffed it into my pocket. This loss felt twice as painful—as a medic and as a detective who should have made sure this didn't happen twice.

"Where are you going?" Max asked as I got up from the bar.

"I'm going back to my room to think. Can we meet in the morning to discuss some theories? I think better when I can say some thoughts out loud."

"Sure thing," he said wearily. "Meet on the patio at nine?"

I shook my head. "I don't want anyone overhearing our talks right now. Come to my room around eight."

"If that's the case, then I should probably go to bed now too," Max grunted, crawling off his stool. "You know, you did your best today. Don't let it get you down."

I sighed. "Thanks. But if that's my best, that's not good enough for me. Rest up, and we'll get a fresh start tomorrow."

I climbed into bed with full intentions of getting a good night of sleep. Unfortunately, my brain had other plans. I lay awake for hours on end, wondering if there was anything I could have done to save Sebastian's life. Suddenly, I was reminded of why I'd stopped working as a medic in the first place.

CHAPTER TWELVE

"**L**et's try this again," I said with my mouth half-full of partially-chewed apple. "Daniel got fed up with everyone partying so he killed off the biggest potential embarrassments to send a message," I said.

"I'm not sure if that works," Max said. He lay on top of my made bed, reclined on a pile of decorative pillows. "Daniel occasionally partakes in certain substances himself. It would be hypocritical to off someone for doing the same. Besides, why would he kill his own brother? You read the note—he's devastated."

"I read a note," I mused. "I didn't see his reaction. Maybe they don't get along as well as they want everyone to think. Daniel is all about appearances, right? Maybe something happened that would potentially embarrass the family name. Maybe there was a messy affair between Sebastian and Dawn and he wanted to end it."

Max shook his head and poked around his breakfast platter with a fork. "He wouldn't do that just to keep people from finding out about it. If anything, it would be out of jealousy."

"That's interesting," I said, writing down a few notes.

"But why would he offer you more money to find the killer if he's the killer?" Max asked, pointing a butter knife in my direction.

I shrugged. "It could show confidence that he's not going to get caught. Or, if I report directly to him, then he'll be one step ahead. Or, it shows that he has nothing to hide and has nothing to do with this. I'm not so sure I like Daniel as a suspect yet. There could be something there, but I'm just not seeing it."

"Okay," Max said, wiggling his toes. "Who is next?"

"Do we go down the line? How about Jamie?"

"You forgot Sebastian."

I gave him a blank look. "The dead one?"

He shrugged. "Why not be thorough?"

I nodded in agreement. I needed someone like Max to look into my blind spots.

"So, we'll say he killed Dawn. Maybe it was an accident, like they were doing drugs and having sex and something went wrong. He panicked and staged it so it looked like she died on her own. Then, someone found out about it and got revenge."

"Or," Max added, "Sebastian felt so guilty about it that he killed himself."

"I'm not so sure about that," I said. "An hour or so before he died, he was grinning from ear to ear. He'd also made plans with me to meet up later."

Max shrugged. "It's not uncommon for people to make plans before dying of suicide," he said. "Perhaps he wanted his family to think he also died of natural causes. Full disclosure, I'm just making an argument so you have options. I don't think he would have killed himself. His ego was too big."

"Jamie," I said, moving on to the next brother. "I really can't see him killing anyone, but let's find a motive. I'd say the fact that his brother is fucking his wife is a good motive for killing Sebastian. I just don't see why he would want to off Dawn."

"Maybe it had something to do with an affair. I mean, if Dawn was separately screwing all the Bergeron brothers, I don't think it would be too farfetched to imagine that Cara was one of her lovers too. Maybe Jamie snapped and got rid of everyone who was fooling around with his wife and making him look like an idiot."

"Interesting," I said. "Do we have any reason to think that Cara and Dawn could have slept together?"

He shook his head. "Not really. I'd heard that Dawn did not limit herself to male partners. I don't know about Cara."

"Well, it's certainly a possibility," I said, adding it to my list. "What about Cara?"

"I could see why she would have a problem with Dawn, but she has no reason to kill Sebastian," Max said. "Besides, did you see how devastated she was about Sebastian?"

I nodded solemnly. That was one of the things I hated most about being an EMT. It was bad enough to see the patient in bad shape, but some of the reactions from loved ones will forever stick in my mind. There's no greater horror than watching someone you care about die.

"Yeah, for someone who has a reputation of being cold and uncaring, she was certainly caring," I replied. "I think she really loved Sebastian."

"I think so too," Max agreed. "Who's next?"

I flipped through my notes. "I–I don't know. I haven't really talked to many other people. I was planning on conducting interviews, but since I've taken on the medic job, I haven't really had time. Besides, it would be suspicious if the medic suddenly went around with a notebook, asking for alibis."

"Sure. Do you have any other ideas about whom you want to talk to?" he asked. "I don't know about you, but I'm starting to get a little worried about the situation."

I frowned. "I'm not sure who to talk to next. What makes you worried?"

He leaned back on my bed, stretching his short legs. "People are going to start panicking. I've seen enough true crime shows to know how this goes. If it's personal, we have no reason to worry. All you have to do to stay safe is not piss off the person who's poisoning people. But what if it's random?"

"Like a spree killer?" I groaned.

He nodded. "Maybe the killer is just a deranged person who's trying to take out as many random people as possible without getting caught."

I rubbed my forehead. "That would complicate things. This person's only motive would be chaos. We'd probably be looking at someone with no stake in the business—someone who doesn't lose if business is bad. There are several hundred people on this island who fit that description, and I've talked to maybe ten of them. How would we possibly catch someone like that? We don't even know what kind of substance is killing these people. It could be pharmaceutical, something crafted on the drug trade, or some obscure plant that doesn't appear to grow on the island. I'm starting to feel like I haven't made a smidgen of progress since I've been here. In fact, I'm more in the weeds than ever before."

"Are you about to lose it?" Max asked.

"Yeah, maybe," I said, my face turning pink. "Why did I think I could ever do this?"

"Relax," Max said. "Eventually, the pieces will come together."

I sighed. It was easy for him to relax. As long as he wasn't a murder target, his life would remain relatively unchanged. Sure, he wanted justice for people he lived beside, but he was just a guy paying an exorbitant amount of money to live in luxury. Of course he would tell me to relax. It was all he did, all day, every day.

I took a deep breath and tried to get my frustration under control. I had to keep trying.

"Okay, if we can't nail down a possible motive or a few good suspects, then let's figure out method of delivery. Am I right in assuming that there are no security checks for guests when they arrive?"

"More or less," he said. "Of course, if I want to go back and forth from here to the mainland, no one even blinks. Security is supposed to be on the lookout for any weapons. When guests arrive by boat, their luggage goes through an x-ray, like the ones you'd find at the airport. They're basically making sure no one brings a gun or an explosive device. Honestly, I think it's more for the guests' peace of mind."

"So, it's conceivable that guests could be smuggling in dangerous substances and it's going unnoticed?"

"Or no one cares," he said.

I scoffed. "So, if it's possible that bad stuff is coming in from the outside, all it would take to find it is a little extra caution?"

"Reasonably, yeah."

I exhaled loudly. "Do you have Daniel's cellphone number?"

Max pulled out his phone and flipped through his contacts list. I typed the number into my phone.

If there's any chance that whatever killed Dawn and Sebastian is coming in from the outside, we need to be more careful. Would it be possible to have security check a little closer for such a thing? If we're dealing with a purposeful poisoning, it's most likely being brought here in cargo or passenger boats.

-John

"HOPEFULLY, HE LISTENS TO ME," I said. "I know it can be easy to smuggle something in, but if security isn't trying, then whoever is doing it has probably let their guard down."

"I hope you're right," Max replied. "I'm curious to see what they find."

"My mind keeps going back to oleander," I said. "I don't know why, but it's the only thing I can think of. Any other drugs would have come up in initial toxicology reports. Does this seem feasible, or am I losing it?"

"I'm sorry I don't know more about it. You know that my specialty is anatomy and physiology. I don't have as much experience with toxicology. I may have learned it at one point, but it's gone."

I figured as much. I found it hard to recall certain things and it hadn't been all that long since I worked as an EMT. Not to mention, I hadn't been drinking daily after quitting the job.

"Why don't you call Carlos?" he suggested. "His lab might not have the results, but he'd be a good reference."

"That's a good idea," I said. "I might try to give him a call right now."

"Good," Max said cheerily. "I'll leave you to that. The pool calls me."

I rolled my eyes. "I'll catch up with you later."

I called my former partner, but he didn't answer his cellphone. Then, I tried the hospital, but was told that he was in a meeting and couldn't be reached.

"Would you like to leave a message for him?" the receptionist asked.

"Uh, sure," I said, feeling a bit awkward. I hadn't kept in great touch with him since our careers had diverged.

After being directed to his answering machine, I left him a short message explaining my situation and asked him to give me a call back if he had any ideas of what I was dealing with. On the phone, I told him it wasn't urgent, though after I hung up, I wished I hadn't added that bit. It was rather urgent.

I was going over my notes when I heard my phone ring. I dashed across the room to grab it, only to find that Marcie was trying to reach me. I ended the call after three rings.

Then, the inevitable texts poured in. In abbreviated sentences, she told me how I had ruined her life by walking out on her. She said she wanted to try to make things right with me, but I was being selfish. When I didn't respond, she feigned concern for my wellbeing, threatening to get the police involved in the search for me if I didn't respond to her. Not wanting to call her bluff and be wrong, I sent her a quick message to shut her up.

I'm working a case. Please leave me alone. You've done enough damage.

Of course, this only fueled a new stream of messages. Now, she was saying that her life was in danger because I left her homeless. I knew this wasn't the case. In fact, I would have bet my paycheck from Daniel that she was in the comfort of her sister's guest room as she wrote the messages. I was getting really tired of her crap.

Then, the phone calls resumed. If she thought she was going to break me down with her persistence, she was wrong. I sent her one more text, telling her that I could not be reached, and turned off my phone. At the very least, she would see that her messages were not being delivered and she would give up.

I was about to leave and do some interviews when my pager began beeping. Reluctantly, I hiked to the medical office to see what I was dealing with. But halfway there, I started to fear the worst. After all, the last time I was in that office, someone in my care was on the brink of death. I jogged the rest of the way, praying that I wouldn't have to deal with another tragedy.

I was never so happy to see someone with a head

cold. After taking the woman's temperature and handing out cold medicine, I disinfected the place with a little peace of mind that the poisoning deaths were an isolated experiment. Then, I talked to a few guests with seasickness and one who had smoked too much weed and was checking in to make sure time was still moving at the correct speed. Then, I chatted to a cook with a burned forearm. From what I could tell, Daniel had yet to formally announce his brother's death to the workers. I thought that was strange, but then I remembered that he was grieving, and it couldn't be easy to deal with a family member's death while rumors were swirling about. Of course, there were already rumors going around about the helicopter landing on the island, but I wasn't going to spill the beans.

Finally, when I had managed to get to a stopping point, I turned my phone back on to see if anyone besides my ex had tried to contact me. Seeing a missed call from Carlos, I called him back, only to find that he was busy again and couldn't take my call.

"Don't worry about it," I said to his receptionist. "I'll try again later."

I hung up the phone, wondering if the pieces of the puzzle would ever come together for me. I felt as though I was waiting on everyone else to do their part and there was hardly anything for me to do.

Before anyone could return to the medical office, I

closed up shop and went down to where all the action was. I needed to dive in, do some interviews, and get my hands dirty. It was the only thing I could think to do. Otherwise, I was just spinning my wheels, grasping wildly for a lead.

CHAPTER THIRTEEN

I t was past the lunch rush, but the kitchen was still buzzing in preparation for the nightly meal. Security guards lingered outside, on high alert after the second death at the resort.

I grabbed a plate at the buffet and wandered around the food line as I peeked into the kitchen. If the two deceased had eaten poisoned food, it couldn't be all that easy for a guest to enter and taint the meal. In fact, it seemed almost impossible for anyone to ensure that the right poison got into the right dish—unless someone in the kitchen or wait staff were involved.

It was an idea that I had been kicking around as I bided my time in the medical office. I had been thinking about different ways to introduce poison into the body, and this was a logical one. I had been so focused on intentional drug use that I hadn't really considered the possibility that it could have been ingested in another way.

It would be somewhat more difficult to poison food or a beverage, but it wasn't completely impossible. As I watched cooks bring out fresh pans of food to set into the buffet table, I observed their routine. There was a small window of time from the time the food was plated until it made its way into the public eye.

At the bar, each drink was made right in front of the customer, but few customers watched intently. Especially in a complicated drink, a splash of a toxic substance could be mistaken for a splash of bitters. But when drinks were served at dinner, they were made away from the diner's eye. Everyone dined with a drink in hand, so this theory wasn't one I was about to dismiss right away. After all, neither body had been found with toxic levels of substances in their bodies. It's hard to cut a drug with poison and not find a trace of that drug in their system.

As I ate my hamburger with French fries, I wondered if the person responsible for their deaths was still out there. Watching people pass by made me rack my brain for a new motive with each individual. My list of possible subjects was both long and short at the same time. No one could really be proven innocent, just as no one seemed particularly guilty.

But I needed to start gathering substantial information from strangers. I had only managed to talk to the power players and not the support staff. Since the employees were known for spreading gossip, I thought someone might know something.

Now, I wished I had my fact sheets that I used when rounding up bail jumpers. I felt as if I were continuously spinning my wheels, finding a lead to grasp onto. So, I grasped onto the first person I saw in the buffet area.

"Do you need anything?" a waiter with a pitcher of water asked me as he gave me a refill.

"Actually, yes," I said, putting on a friendly smile. "I'm trying to get to know people around the resort. I'm the new medic."

"I've heard about you," the waiter said with what I thought was a sly smile. "Sure, what do you want to know?"

I shrugged innocently. "What's it like to work here?"

He smiled. "I enjoy meeting new guests. People have interesting stories."

"What kinds of stories?" I asked. "What's the best one you've heard?"

The young man thought for a moment before a wide grin came to his face.

"Well, I met a bunch of swingers on their first vacation together. Every night, they would sit down together as one big group, but every night, they would leave with a different partner. The wait staff liked to take bets on who would leave with whom. I had a good sense for it, so I made an extra hundred bucks that week. I guess that was why it was so memorable to me."

"I've heard that people are crazy here." I chuckled. "I guess I really have no idea."

"Probably not," he said.

"Any advice for me?"

He looked over his shoulder. "Don't get carried away. This place has a way of bringing out the wildest side of people. I stay focused because I'm saving up to go to college and the pay is pretty good for a waiter."

"I don't plan on staying long," I said. "You know, I've been hearing a lot of rumors about some of the people who work here. What do you know about that?"

He shrugged. "Which rumor? There are millions out there. If you're wondering if we're getting three extra vacation days this year, I doubt it."

I nodded, though it wasn't the particular rumor I was hoping for.

"I have to get back to work," he said, glancing back toward the kitchen. "We're short staffed today. Sometimes, people get so carried away they don't show up for their shift. It was nice speaking with you. It's a strange lifestyle, but I'm sure you'll get the hang of how things work around here."

"Thanks," I said, lifting my full water glass.

I spotted one of the restaurant managers sitting at a lone table with a glass of lemonade and a stack of papers. He looked somewhat busy, but I thought I would risk it and try to have a word with him.

"Hey, George, is it?" I said, grabbing the seat next to him. I caught his name on the shiny gold name tag affixed to the front of his uniform.

"How can I help you, John?" he asked. I was a little surprised that he knew my name.

"Oh, I've just got some down time and I wanted to talk to some of my colleagues. Am I bothering you?"

"Not at all," he said cheerily. "I'm just going over some menus for the upcoming months." He was a hefty man, and the legs of the chair squealed against the concrete as he scooted over to make room for me to join him.

"Have you heard about Sebastian?" I asked conspiratorially. "Awful, isn't it?"

"Oh, it's terrible," he said emphatically, his beady black eyes widening. "First Dawn, and now Sebastian. I liked his style. I wish I could get the girls like he did, but he was a good man. Were you there when he passed?"

I shook my head. "No, he was still breathing when we sent him out in the helicopter."

"Were his brothers there at least? I know they were close."

"Cara was with him. She was pretty devastated. I guess even the in-laws were close."

He must have known what I was hinting at. He pursed his lips as I brought up Cara and Sebastian's affair rumors.

"I know Cara isn't the most popular person around here, but I like her," he said. "She's always been sweet to me."

A cook rushed up to George and muttered something in his ear. He looked at his watch and sighed.

"Tell them to check again," he muttered.

"What was that about?" I asked.

"One of my servers didn't show up for her shift. I had someone check her room, but she's not there."

"Does that happen a lot here?"

"Not this girl. She's younger and it's her first job. She's really eager to do a good job and wouldn't mess up her chance of a future promotion. I've never had a problem with her before. In fact, she's one of my favorites. I hope she isn't sick or something."

"If she is, she hasn't come to see me," I said.

He shook his head. "She'll show up. Anyway, what was I saying before?"

"Something about Cara."

"Right. I don't think it was ever Cara's dream to

stay here this long. I think she prefers to be in big cities. With so much else going on, she doesn't get the attention she wants. She wants to be seen, but everyone here is so wrapped up in their own fantasies that she goes unnoticed."

"Who does she want to notice her?" I asked.

"Men, I suppose. She wears these beautiful, expensive outfits, but everyone's eyes are on the girls who drunkenly whip their breasts out by the bar. She's too sophisticated for this place."

"I'm sure she feels the same way," I muttered, remembering how snobby she was toward me.

George sat up in his seat a little straighter when another restaurant manager walked by.

"Find her yet?" he called out. The manager shook his head in response.

"What does your server look like?" I asked.

"She's a gorgeous young woman," he said. "She's tall and slender, has that smooth, mocha skin, and her hair is done in long, skinny braids."

I furrowed my brow as I imagined her in my mind. The description sounded so familiar, but I couldn't place where I saw her.

"Oh, I remember her," I exclaimed. "She was waiting tables on the night that I came to the dining room. Cara wasn't very nice to her then. I thought she seemed a little demanding."

"I think Cara is prone to stress," he said, defending his friend. "She rubs a lot of people the wrong way because she's a perfectionist. But once you get to know her, you'll find that she's not so bad. In the end, you have to remember that she's a partial owner of this place through marriage. If things go wrong around here and guests aren't satisfied, that hurts her husband's equity. She likes to put special touches on things around here, and I think it's nice that she cares so much."

"What kinds of special touches?" I asked.

"Sometimes, she'll make recommendations for the menus," he said, gesturing to his stack of papers. "She'll travel to another city for a few days and come back with ideas. After a trip to Paris, we hired a French pastry chef and the guests really like the selection of breads and desserts. Sometimes, she'll even come into the kitchen and help me cook. She's not an employee, but I think she gets bored and wants to learn new skills. Honestly, I wish I could hire her on. She's gotten pretty good and isn't afraid to get dirty. After all, she did learn from the best."

He laughed at his little joke. I had a feeling that Cara must have done some serious sweet-talking to George to get him to like her so much. Or, she had a kind side of her that I had yet to see in person.

One of the security guards returned to our table

with a concerned look on his face. George's happy-go-lucky demeanor changed again. I had yet to see this man look worried.

"We did a pretty thorough search of anywhere Amy would likely be," the guard said. "Do you think it's possible that she went back to the mainland on a passenger boat and we just didn't notice?"

I raised my eyebrows. Not only was it concerning that someone could just disappear so easily from the island, but it was even more concerning that a restaurant employee would vanish after the death of someone who had eaten before falling fatally ill.

I scrambled to come up with a motive for this young waitress. Perhaps she had also been sleeping with Sebastian. If she'd found out about Dawn and gotten jealous, she might be able to poison her food between the time it was put on the plate and when it was served. And if Sebastian did something to upset her in that time period, it didn't seem too farfetched that she would eliminate him too. Then, to escape investigation, she went to the mainland, making her harder to track down.

From what George told me, this Amy woman was beautiful. I could see a scenario where she might catch Sebastian's eye and prove to be irresistible. But she was young and fell for his charming ways, thinking that his interest in her was purely romantic, not just sexual.

Upon finding out about another woman, she went into a rage. She had been so hurt and embarrassed by the end of her first love that she wanted to remove anyone who'd caused her such emotional trauma. It was dramatic, but it was plausible.

"I'm going to join the search," I said as I got up from the table.

"You don't have to do that," George said. "We have guards who can do that. You shouldn't have to cover for someone else's mistake."

I smiled politely. "Well, in the event that she really is sick, I should be nearby. It was nice talking to you, George. I'll see you later."

"Good luck," he said. "I hope you track her down. She's one of the good ones."

I pulled out my notebook and wrote down a few thoughts on Amy before making my way down to the beach. I needed to speak with Amy. I had a sneaking suspicion that she knew something about the deaths and was trying to hide her secrets.

CHAPTER FOURTEEN

I could feel my skin sizzling as I walked along the water's edge, combing one side of the resort. The island itself wasn't very big, yet there was land that wasn't covered by the resort. It reminded me of the out of bounds areas at ski resorts. It was owned by the Bergerons, but there was no reason for any guest to walk along the rocky crag. Once I got to the barrier, I returned to the service road, sweat pouring down my back with every step.

For the first time since I arrived, I genuinely wanted to leave. Even after growing up in Florida, I had yet to learn my lesson about spending time in the hot sun. If I had any good sense, I would have moved to Alaska years ago.

As a child, I learned that the summers were not for me. When the sun was at its hottest, I took refuge indoors beside the air conditioner vents. My mom smeared thick sunscreen on my face just to go to the grocery store. She never pushed me out to play when the sun was beating down. After all, it was partially her fault that I had such lily-white skin and ginger hair.

My dad used to tell me to toughen up and get a base tan so I wouldn't have to spend my nights wincing with every moment because my skin was blistered. I don't think he understood that my skin physically didn't tan. It only burned, then blistered, then turned back to white. I used to think I wanted to join the army when I was older so I could be like him, but after hearing stories about being in the desert, I decided that it was best to have a job that allowed me to stay mostly under cover from the sun.

As I hiked the stairs leading to the front office, I heard a booming voice from behind me

"We need some help over here!"

I whipped around and started jogging to the cliff. I had heard that call before, and it was always a medical emergency. I didn't have any of my supplies, so once I assessed the situation, I would have to send someone to my office. I didn't even know what I was getting into, but I was already kicking myself for not being prepared.

"What's going on?" I panted at the security guard.

I followed him and heard him mutter all sorts of codes into his walkie-talkie.

At the bottom of the cliff lay the broken body of a tall, yet slight, young woman. Her limbs were bent at unnatural angles and blood spread out from under her head like a halo.

"Shit," I muttered under my breath, looking for a way down the steep rocks. I took a step forward, but my foot slid on the pebbles and nearly caused me to skid out.

"Careful," the guard said. "I think we're going to have to go around this way," he said, pointing to a longer route to the bottom.

"Can you call a helicopter and some more back-up?" I asked frantically. "I need my supplies."

"Already did," he said. I could see more men dressed in black polo shirts running our direction. I wasn't sure if we would all make it in time.

I followed the guards down to the bottom of the cliff, nearly losing my shoe when my foot got stuck between two sharp rocks. I had to slow down and be careful—if I fell and seriously injured myself, there would be no one left to rescue me.

It took me no time at all to assess the fact that Amy's injuries were not compatible with life. Just by tilting her head to the side, I could see that the back of her skull had caved in from the impact. Blood pooled in her eyes, ears, and nose. I gently pressed my fingertips to her throat to feel for a pulse, but there was nothing. I could not feel her breath on my palm when I held it directly in front of her face.

"Don't touch her," I commanded to the guards, who looked thoroughly startled. "Once this is reported, the police will come and want to investigate. It's best if your DNA is nowhere near her."

When someone came with my pack of supplies, I pulled on a pair of latex gloves and did a rough examination. Her shoulder was dislocated and a compound fracture poked out of her shin. The blood around her head was beginning to dry in the hot sun, causing flies to appear. I waved as many away as I could, but it was no use. If the authorities didn't arrive soon, we would have a bigger mess on our hands.

I leaned over the body to check for any other injuries unrelated to the fall. That's when I smelled the faint stench of alcohol. I had a feeling that her toxicology report would show alcohol in her system.

"Do people normally walk along the cliffs?" I asked, feeling dismayed at the tragedy. "Why weren't there ropes up there to stop her?"

A guard frowned. "There are," he said. "You stood right next to one when we found the body."

"Oh," I said, feeling foolish. I guess I hadn't noticed.

"I don't know why, but she clearly jumped the ropes."

I inhaled sharply. Suicide came to mind. If my theory about Amy's jealousy was correct, then perhaps the guilt and shame caused her to get wasted and throw herself off a cliff. If this were the case, the tragedy would end here. While suicide would be a neat ending to a horrible story, I couldn't help but wonder if it was too convenient. What if Amy knew something about the other deaths and had to be silenced?

"The police are on their way," a guard announced. "Everyone who was present is going to have to give a statement. In the meantime, please do not discuss this with anyone besides authority figures. This week has been hard enough already. We need the guests to know that they are safe."

I sighed. I wasn't sure whether the guests were safe.

"I'm going to talk to the restaurant managers," I said. "If the police want to talk to me, you know where to find me."

Feeling sick to my stomach, I scrambled back up the jagged rocks, back to the sidewalk. The sky had turned overcast as the waves beat against the rocks. Suddenly, everything wasn't so sunny. I could hear the chopper overhead and wondered if Daniel would be receiving a discount for calling in so many helicopters.

George was exactly where I'd left him, sipping lemonade and scribbling on a piece of yellow notebook paper. I didn't want to be the one to break the news, but I felt as though it was part of my duty.

"George," I said gently as I pulled a chair out to sit across from him.

He frowned. He could already tell that something was up.

"What's wrong?" he asked.

I bit my lip. "Amy was found at the bottom of the cliff on the west side of the island. She's dead, George."

His beady eyes blinked a few times before turning misty. "What? No. How is this possible?"

I swallowed hard. "We don't know what happened. She was at the bottom of the cliff and her injuries suggest a fall."

"Oh, that poor, sweet thing," he whimpered. "She was a sweetheart. I can't believe it."

I leaned in a little closer, not wanting anyone else to hear our conversation until her death was made known among the staff. I didn't want to spread panic if I could help it.

"Do you—do you know if she had a drinking problem?" I asked. "It's possible that she was intoxicated when she fell."

He shook his head. "No, not that I'm aware of. She's always been very professional around me."

"She's a minor, right? Is it easy for minors to get alcohol around here?"

"The bartenders know better. For the most part, I think they're pretty good about making sure the booze doesn't fall into the wrong hands. Of course, if a minor were to really try, they could get some. I've just never seen her drink before."

"Did you know her well?"

He shrugged. "She was new, but we talked occasionally. She seemed like a really good girl. She always did exactly what I asked her to do. She was a quick learner and always showed up on time and stayed late when needed."

"Did she seem happy?" I asked.

He furrowed his brow. "She was always smiling around me. Why?"

I shook my head. Never mind that. I'm just trying to make sense of this."

"Do you think it was an accident?"

I shrugged. "I don't know her well enough to know. Is there anyone else here who was close to her? Any friends? Enemies? Who would know something about her to help us understand?"

He thought for a moment. "Honestly, I have no idea. Amy was great, but she was quiet. Always friendly to everyone, but I don't think she had any friends here yet. After all, she'd only been here for a few weeks. I think she was just focused on learning her way around the job and wanting to make a good impression."

"Do you mind if I have a word with some of the restaurant staff? I just can't help but wonder if someone saw or heard something."

"Go ahead," he said mournfully, gesturing toward the kitchen. "Talk to whomever you want."

"Thanks," I said with a nod before walking through the swinging kitchen doors. I hardly knew where to start, so I chose subjects by proximity.

"Hey, I have a question for you," I said timidly to a prep cook who was chopping carrots. He looked nervous to be approached by someone he didn't know, but he set his knife down and looked at me.

"Uh, do you know Amy, the server?" I asked.

He pursed his lips and shook his head. "Not really. I heard she might have skipped town back to the mainland."

I sighed, relieved that the news hadn't spread yet but also perturbed at the rate false information had spread.

"Do you know anyone who might know her?"

He turned around and scanned the kitchen before calling out to his co-workers.

"Hey, does anyone here know that missing waitress?"

I waited for a response, but no one answered. I found it hard to believe that no one knew anything. Someone at this resort was hiding something.

"We're just trying to figure out why she didn't report to work today," I explained now that everyone was staring at me. "If you have any little piece of information about her, it might help us answer that question. Of course, nothing that you tell me will get you into trouble. We just want to know what's up with her."

Still, no one spoke up. I rubbed at my temples. I was getting nowhere.

"Did she even exist?" I asked exasperatedly. It was as if the girl was a ghost.

"I talked to her a few times," a waitress said. She dusted the salt and pepper from her hands as she refilled bottles.

"Great," I said, pulling out my notebook. "What was your overall impression of her?"

"I liked her. I thought she was smart and funny. I want to say she was trying to save up money to send to her family back home, but I don't really remember."

"I worked with her too," another waiter chimed in. "She covered one of my shifts when I went home to visit my family," he said. "She was a hard worker and the guests seemed to like her."

Another waiter agreed. "I don't know anything

about her personal life, but something bad must have happened if she just left without telling anyone. Maybe it was a family emergency and there was no time to explain."

"Any rumors?" I asked.

Everyone stared at me with blank faces. I guess that answered that question.

"Is she in trouble?" someone asked.

"I'm sure everything will be fine," I said, feigning optimism. "Thanks for your help. If you know anything else, don't hesitate to come speak with me. I appreciate your cooperation."

My smile fell as I left the kitchen. I was hoping someone would have some useful information. Even the smallest tip could produce a lead. All I knew was that she was a nice girl who had only been working there a short time. It didn't appear that she had any enemies. At the very least, she'd kept her affairs private.

Still, if anything were going on, someone would have spread that information like wildfire. So, I was starting to think that someone had it out for the girl, or she was in the wrong place at the wrong time. I just needed to find out who would want to hurt a poor waitress before someone else got hurt.

At the same time, I felt terrible for lying straight to her coworkers' faces. In minutes, they would likely be questioned by officials. It didn't appear as though anyone knew her well, but I had a feeling this would be another devastating blow in a long line of loss. The police would come in and hopefully try to find justice for Amy. But who knows if they would stick around long enough to find it? I, on the other hand, was now fully focused on the case. Whatever was causing these deaths was going to stop. I wasn't going to leave the island until I figured it out.

CHAPTER FIFTEEN

Word about Amy's death must have spread quickly because everywhere I looked, I saw employees gathered with their heads together. I wondered what they were saying. No one was eager to give official statements, yet everyone whispered among themselves when they thought no one was looking.

Within just hours, investigators from the Florida Sheriff's Department had taken pictures, pulled evidence, and bagged the body. Word was, the police officers had immediately called it a suicide, though they would have to do some testing before notating that on the death certificate.

I had to sit with an officer in my medical office and give a statement on everything I knew about the death. It was embarrassing to reveal that I had been hired on as a private investigator, yet I knew very little about Amy's fate. I tried to be as thorough and cooperative as possible, but my answers to their questions fell flat. I could only tell them that she was discovered on the beach below the steep cliff and that I smelled booze on her breath.

I wasn't asked about the other recent deaths, so I didn't bring them up. As far as the police were concerned, the other two had died of natural causes. Only I knew that there was nothing natural about the way they'd died. I realized that it was probably in everyone's best interest if the police knew the whole story so they could open a wider investigation, but self- ishly, I wanted them to leave so I could get back to work. I had a gut feeling that if they were involved, they would come to the wrong conclusion. Then, if I disagreed with them, there would be nothing to do to change minds. After all, I was just a private eye.

Thankfully, I got my wish. After her body was zipped into a bag and taken away, custodial crews washed the blood from the beach. The waitress had gone relatively unnoticed during her time at the resort, and now she would likely be forgotten.

Unsure of what else do to with my remaining daylight hours, I thought I'd swing by the greenhouse again to double-check for oleander. Because the restau- rant staff frequently used fresh herbs in their cooking, it seemed reasonable that someone like Amy would have been sent to get ingredients.

When I got outside, I heard raised voices, so naturally, I lurked outside and listened. It didn't take long for me to realize that it was an argument between Jamie and Cara.

"You don't care that he's gone," Cara wailed.

"Of course I do," Jamie said mournfully. "He was my brother. Of course I'm upset."

"You've just been in here, planting your stupid seeds."

Jamie scoffed. "What the hell am I supposed to do? Do you want me to put on a black veil and lock myself in my room all day?"

"I don't know, but your playing around in here all the time doesn't seem like the right way to act when something tragic has happened."

"I like being alone in here," Jamie shouted. "Keeping busy makes me feel better. I've never lost a close family member before. Being able to work with my plants helps me process everything that happened. Do you want me to be miserable?"

I felt uncomfortable listening to their fight. I had been in quite a few quarrels with Marcie, and I would have been mortified if anyone had heard any of my conversations. They always seemed so important at the time, but in hindsight, they were so damn stupid.

One time, Marcie was noticeably upset. I asked her what was wrong, and she said that nothing was wrong and she was fine. So, I didn't press the matter. If she wanted to talk about what was bothering her, I figured she'd say so.

Apparently, that was a mistake. She only became surlier with me until I finally pried it out of her. I guess she was upset because she wanted me to go to her parents' house for their family's Thanksgiving when I'd already told my parents I would visit them. We lived together at the time, but we weren't so serious that we couldn't do our own thing with our own families.

But I had made the mistake of not correctly guessing what she'd wanted in the first place. Then, I didn't immediately pry the information out of her or guess why she was upset. I just let her stew until she came to the conclusion that I was a horrible boyfriend who didn't really want to be in a relationship.

Eventually, the situation blew over. To keep the peace, I went to her parents' house and cancelled on my family. I was apathetic and she was placated. We made up and the fight was completely forgotten, save for the rare instances where a new fight would bring up old arguments.

That's not to say that I never had a fault of my own. I would go on jobs and forget to call and let her know that I wouldn't be home in time for supper. I'd retreat into the bedroom and watch movies on my laptop when she wanted to watch TV with me on the couch. I downplayed her emotions on a near-constant basis. I could have been better to her.

That's why it felt so wrong to make judgments about Jamie and Cara's relationship when I was dealing with the aftermath of my failing relationship. Couples were bound to fight every once in a while, and it wasn't my place to be alarmed by a little quarrel. Still, interesting information had its way of coming out during an altercation, so I stuck around for a little while longer.

"I don't know what you want from me, Cara," Jamie said exasperatedly.

"I don't know what I want from you either," she said icily.

"What's that supposed to mean?"

She huffed. "Sometimes, I wish I had married the other brother. Sebastian cared about me. He was attentive and loving and put my needs first. You only care about those kids and your stupid plants."

"You want to talk about the affair?" he scoffed. "Sure. I wasn't going to bring it up, but let's talk about it. How do you think I felt when I found out that you were fucking my brother?"

"You fucked the nurse," she retorted.

"And I thought we were going to move past that. You wanted me to stop, so I did. Let's not forget that you were the one who suggested we have an open marriage. Besides, it was always just sex with Dawn. We were friends with benefits. We didn't have a romantic bond—not like you had with Sebastian. I didn't like it, but I wasn't going to make a scene about it. You would have just called me a hypocrite, and I would have risked losing both you and Sebastian. I figured if he could satisfy you in the way you wanted, you would be happier with me. Obviously, that's not the case. Oh, and don't bring the kids into this," he added. "They've done nothing wrong here."

My hand involuntarily covered my mouth. Apparently, the rumors were true. I had some new motives I needed to unpack.

"I bet you wish I were dead instead," Jamie said darkly. "That way, you could have all of my money and my brother. That's all you really want out of me at this point, right? You just want my money."

I listened closely, but I didn't hear a response from her. One might take her silence as an affirmative response, but I couldn't pass those judgments as an investigator.

"I want this to work," he said, a little softer this time. "I'd like to have a happy family with the kids and the big house. You don't seem interested in any of that."

"Well, you're not really giving me that, are you?" she asked. "We're living at a vacation resort like peasants, and the only kids you want to give me are someone else's rejects."

"Don't talk about them that way," he bellowed. "They already have better manners and morals than you ever will. You may look the part, but you'll never have class. Why do I try with you?"

"You're drunk," she said. "You're drunk and being stupid."

"You're a cokehead," he retorted. "Whatever diet pills you're on are fucking with your head. You're insane. You're not the woman I married."

"I've had enough of this conversation," she said. "I'm going back to my home. When you've slept this off, you can come apologize to me. If you want the jeweler to make me something, you'd better do it before the storm hits and the boats leave us stranded on this godforsaken island."

I practically dove into the bushes to hide from Cara. She was already paranoid about my presence, and sneaking around to hear her private arguments with her husband wasn't the best way to build rapport. I waited until she stomped down the sidewalk in her stilettos and was safely out of the way before I climbed out of the shrubbery.

Dusting myself off, I knocked on the door to the greenhouse. Jamie opened it with trembling hands.

"Did you hear that?" he asked in a husky voice.

"Hear what?" I asked innocently.

He shook his head. "Nothing. I'm not feeling very well, and I don't think I'm up to talking. I hate to be rude, but do you mind if I go back to my cabin?"

"Go ahead," I said, feeling somewhat sorry for Jamie. He looked rough, as though he hadn't slept for days and had been drinking like a fish. When he passed by me, he reeked of booze and sweat. "I'm not sure I can say anything to make any of this better," I said, "but if you want, I'm here to listen."

"Thanks," he slurred. "Maybe tomorrow."

Once he left, I checked the greenhouse door. Somehow, he had been lucid enough to lock it behind him. I would have to do my double-check in the morning. Feeling absolutely exhausted, I decided to retreat to my room for a quick rest before checking out the bar scene to ask a few questions. However, I felt like I was on the verge of narrowing my search.

Now, I just had to figure out how Dawn, Sebastian, and Amy were connected. The first two seemed pretty obvious, but I was starting to wonder if Amy was part of the open relationship Jamie was referencing. I made a note to ask him about her when the time was right.

I had a hard time believing what George had said about Cara being a decent person. She basically told her husband that she wished he had died instead of his brother and that she was in love with Sebastian, arguably more so than she was with her husband. If Cara had reason to, I could imagine her causing great harm to people. I just wasn't exactly sure why she might want to hurt Amy.

On the other hand, I could also see how Jamie might get drunk and do things he regretted later. He seemed to handle stress by drinking himself stupid. He seemed like a mellow guy, but then again, I hadn't heard him scream like he did at his wife. Someone who could conjure up that much rage might be liable to act out, especially when he wasn't in his right mind.

I'd sit him down for a heart to heart eventually. With my relationship failure and his turbulent marriage, I might be able to get close enough to see the really messy parts. Until then, I'd just have to continue talking to clueless staff and guests until someone gave me something remotely useful.

Or, perhaps I was the useless one. I had yet to experience a case I couldn't crack somewhat easily. If I had to return to the mainland without a penny in my pocket and a deep sense of shame, I don't think I could return to my work. I would be exposed as a fraud. But at least I had the option of working as a medic on a resort. It was one of the last jobs I would ever choose to have, but at least it was an option. And on the bright side, it would be somewhere Marcie couldn't bother me. Perhaps it wasn't such a bad plan if things didn't pan out here.

No, it was too soon to feel defeated. I was just starting to get a feel for the place. If I had to go home, it would only be because the killer had gotten to me before I got to them.

CHAPTER SIXTEEN

I went out later that night to talk to employees, but no one wanted to talk to me. Apparently, word got around that I was asking a lot of questions, and this caused people around the resort to clam up. The mood surrounding the employees was noticeably dour, though they did their best to hide it from the guests.

Frustrated by my lack of leads, I retreated to my room for the night. Perhaps everyone just needed a little time and space to come to terms with the tragedies before I came in and asked a bunch of prying questions.

I was watching the news when my phone rang. I let it ring a few times, assuming it was Marcie with her usual nonsense. But when I glanced over at the caller ID, I noticed it was a call from a restricted number.

"Hello?" I grunted, having jumped from one side of the bed to the other to reach the phone.

"John!" a familiar voice said warmly from the other end of the line. "I'm sorry I haven't been able to reach you."

"Good to hear from you, Carlos," I said. "It sounds like you've been busy lately."

"I have been. You wouldn't believe how many overdoses we see these days. I've been developing a protocol to distribute to all the local law enforcement. And for some reason, I've been dealing with a lot of venomous snake bites. On top of all of that, I have sick kids and my wife can only miss so many days at work. I had to bring one of them to the hospital and put her in my office. It wasn't ideal, but I think things are finally getting better."

"I feel bad for calling so many times, then," I said sheepishly.

"It's no problem. So, what did you say you were doing?"

I sighed. "I don't know how to begin to get you up to speed. Max called me with a job a few days ago."

"Really?" Carlos laughed. "I can't imagine what that was."

"I'm sure you can," I replied. "He brought me out to his little island home to figure out why their former medic died. She was fairly young and she just dropped dead. Occasional drug user, but no signs of an overdose."

"What did the medical examiner say?"

"Cardiac arrest. I haven't heard anything more since then. She didn't seem particularly pleased to be there, nor did she appreciate Max and me trying to offer a diagnosis."

"So, you don't buy it?"

"At the time, maybe," I said. "Now, I'm pretty confident it was something else. A few days later, another guy dropped dead the exact same way. He was also too young for a heart attack. Coincidentally, they were likely having an affair. My gut instinct leads me to believe the deaths are absolutely connected."

"You're kidding! You think they were murdered?"

"It's looking that way. The typical toxicology screenings have been turning up negative. His autopsy probably isn't finished yet. Hers showed nothing of use."

"Damn," he replied, drawing out the word. "They just dropped dead? No other symptoms?"

"Well, the second one was alive when he was airlifted out of here. He complained of stomach pain and vomiting before he went unconscious. Not long after, he was dead."

"Huh," Carlos mused. "That makes me wonder if some kind of poison was used. Cyanide could cause a burning stomach pain. However, I don't know how someone would get cyanide on your island without anyone noticing."

"It's not completely out of the question," I said. "Luckily, they've tightened up security since. They're actually performing bag checks now."

"That's good," he replied. "Do you happen to have a sample of the victim's blood? I can try to get an analysis of it."

My face fell. "I had a sample sent days ago."

"That was you?" he exclaimed. "Shit, the identifying labels must have gotten lost somewhere between your island and my desk. I only received a random vial of blood next to all my other samples. I'm sure that was the one."

I breathed a sigh of relief. "Do you think you could take a look at it?"

"Oh, I already did." He chuckled. "I just didn't have a name to write on the report. Give me a second to find Jane Doe."

I leaned back on the bed, feeling shaky. If my only blood sample had been lost, I don't know what I would have done. This was the moment of truth. Once I figured out how they died, I might have a chance to figure out who did it.

"I've got it right here," he said breathlessly. I heard papers ruffling in the background.

"Tell me something good," I muttered under my breath.

"Okay, is this the young woman you were telling me about?"

"Yep. Her name is Dawn."

I heard him scrawl her name on the top of the sheet. "Okay, let's see here. It appears she was on an estrogen birth control pill. Her iron was a little low, but not to the point where she might notice. I'm guessing she was a vegetarian."

"I don't know, honestly," I said. I truly didn't know much about Dawn besides her reputation.

"She had some alcohol in her system, but not a high enough level to even feel tipsy. She probably had a beer a few hours before she passed."

"Does your test work for poisons?" I asked hopefully.

"A few," he said as he flipped through his report. "Ah, well, it doesn't look like my cyanide theory holds any weight," he said, sounding disappointed. "If there was a lethal dose in her body, I would know about it."

"Damn," I muttered. "Any other poisons?"

"Not any that I test for. I run your typical intoxicants. That covers things like meth, heroin, alcohol, and anything else that will make a person feel good. Then, I run another lab for infections and nutrient deficiencies, that sort of thing. She appears to be in good health from her labs. Then, I look for a few things like toxic mold, household poisons, and other common ways one could die. That test showed nothing. I'll email you a copy so you can see exactly what was on there."

"Thanks," I said. "Was oleander on that test?"

"Oleander? Isn't that a flower?"

"A toxic one. I remember reading about it once, and it's been stuck in my head."

"No, I didn't test for that. But if you give me a few days, I could develop a test for it. At the very least, I could probably find another lab that can test for it."

"Sure, if you can," I said.

"This resort doesn't serve blowfish improperly, does it?" he asked.

"I really don't think so," I replied. "I'm sure someone would have mentioned it to me. Both of the victims died after dinner. I actually ate at the table over from one of the victims on the night he died. No one else seemed to be effected by whatever it was that killed him. I think someone is poisoning the food."

"Then as a word of advice, stick to packaged food," he replied.

I snorted. "I'll be fine."

"You don't sound fine."

I chewed on the inside of my cheek. "I don't mean

to sound ungrateful, but I'm just disappointed with the results. It's not your fault, of course. I'm just stumped."

"It sounds like a difficult diagnosis," he agreed. "Has Max come up with any good theories?"

"Even when he's sober, he's stumped by this one," I said. "He tells me that he's forgotten everything about toxic substances."

"That happens when you don't use that information on a regular basis," Carlos replied. "I'm sure he'd be appalled by some of the things I've forgotten, and I wasn't in school all that long ago."

"What else could cause someone to just drop dead after dinner?" I asked, mostly speaking to myself.

"I think you're on the right track," he reassured me. "When I have some free time, I'll see what I can find out about oleander."

"And maybe it's not specifically oleander," I said, backpedaling. "A lot of plants are grown onsite. I just want to know of one that can stop a heart in a matter of hours."

"I'll see what I can find. Anything else going on in your life?"

I thought about bringing up the drama with Marcie, but I wasn't in the mood for anyone's pity. I could tell him about that later.

"Nothing but this case."

"Well, good luck with that. I'd better go home

before I miss supper again. If there's anything else I can help you with, let me know. I can't promise that I'll get back to you immediately, but I will get back to you. Give Max my best."

"I shall," I said. "He'll be happy to hear that one of his former students is a big shot."

"Yeah, tell him that." Carlos laughed. "Talk to you soon."

"Bye," I muttered before hanging up. I tossed my phone onto the chair and flopped back onto the bed. I was really counting on Carlos to give me a definitive answer. In my mind, he was going to tell me the exact poison used to kill Dawn and Sebastian so I could have good reason to have the whole resort searched. Now, I could only confirm what the medical examiner had already told Daniel—Dawn wasn't on drugs when she died.

I pulled out my laptop and tried to do some of my own research on poisonous plants, but the internet was so slow it was useless to me. I called the front office from my phone in my room to see what was up.

"This occasionally happens when it's about to storm," an apologetic receptionist said. "Between the weather and heavy usage, it can cause a lot of delays."

I snorted. I supposed word about the third death was making its rounds and everyone was trying to look up articles to give them more information about it. That, or they were looking for a way off the island.

"Do you know when it might be useable again?" I asked. "I was expecting an email and trying to do some research."

"It could be a while," she said. "We're doing everything we can to lessen this inconvenience."

"Thanks," I said before hanging up. It was one thing to be without internet on vacation. It was another to be without it during an investigation. With nothing else to do, I ripped out a few pieces of notebook paper and stuck them on the table. Then, I wrote out a list with every reason Cara was and wasn't a top suspect.

On the pros column, I listed that she generally rubbed people the wrong way, she was jealous of Dawn, she occasionally hung out with George in the kitchen, and she had problems with her marriage. Then, in the cons column, I wrote Sebastian's name. It was clear to me that Cara loved Sebastian. When he was fighting for his life in my office, I could tell she was truly shaken. No, there was no way around it in my mind. Unless I found out something to contradict her apparent feelings for Sebastian, there was no way she was the prime suspect. She was a nasty woman, but I don't think she could have ever killed Sebastian. Now, if Jamie was the one dead, that would be a different story.

I crumpled up the piece of paper and tossed it into the trash. Then, I made a list for Jamie. He had also been involved with Dawn. And he was pissed off at his wife for her affair with his brother. However, it didn't seem like he had been angry with Sebastian for it. On the cons side, I wrote about his seemingly healthy relationship with his brother and his mistress. He only spoke warmly about Dawn. I didn't really have a good motive for either of those deaths unless I had yet to see his true feelings about the deceased.

I tossed that paper in the trash as well. Amy remained a big question mark, as I didn't see a connection between her and anyone else at the resort. That, and the death was completely different. Still, I couldn't help but feel like it was connected to the others. How could a resort go from zero deaths in years to three in a week?

By the time I started on a list for the kitchen staff, my eyes had started to droop. I crawled into bed and thought about my brief interviews before drifting off to sleep.

What felt like just seconds after I closed my eyes, I had a dream that I was being fed a flower from an oleander plant. I tried to keep my lips pursed, but a faceless figure kept insisting I eat it. I fought for some time before coming to the realization that my murderer is Marcie. When her face became clear, I gasped and the flower entered my mouth, causing me to retch and sputter.

I woke up, absolutely soaked with sweat and shaking. I turned on the lamp to ensure that Marcie was nowhere near. When I firmly grounded myself in reality, I lay back down on my pillow and took deep breaths. Perhaps the case was getting to me. I thought back to what Carlos said about being careful with my meals. I laughed it off at first, but now I was starting to wonder if I should take him more seriously. After all, people knew that I was snooping around, trying to gain information about people's personal lives. Was I a potential target? I had been thinking about the motives for killing others for so long that I never stopped to think about someone's motive for my murder. I was in the process of revealing someone's deepest, darkest secret. That was a good motive if I ever saw one.

CHAPTER SEVENTEEN

"There's some crazy weather headed our way," a guest said to me as I plucked thorns from his hand. I needed to suggest to Jamie that having sharp plants near the staircases was a bad idea with so many drunks around.

"That's what I hear. Don't worry, you'll be perfectly safe here."

"I'm leaving today anyway."

"Did you have a nice time?" I asked, making small talk.

He nodded. "It was fun. I've never vacationed like this before. I mean, I could probably do without having state troopers interview me after smoking a joint, but other than that, I had a great time."

I raised my eyebrows in surprise. "You were interviewed?"

"Yeah. I was on the beach and this guy in a uniform came up to me. It scared the shit out of me. I had always heard that anything goes here, so I was freaked out to see the cops. They didn't want anything to do with me, though. They wanted to know if I had seen some waitress. She died, didn't she?"

I was about to lie to the guest, but he was leaving anyway. By now, the news had picked up on the story.

"Yeah. She fell from the top of a cliff."

The guest gave a low whistle. "Yikes. I don't know about you, but I'm glad I'm not going to be on a haunted island during a hurricane."

I gave him a funny look. "What makes you think it's haunted?"

He shrugged. "It could just be the weed talking, but I got a funny feeling after talking to that cop."

"How so?" I asked as I disinfected his hand and wrapped a bandage around it.

"I don't know—just a creepy vibe."

I tried not to roll my eyes directly in front of the guest. "I see."

After sending the hippy guest on his way, one of the front desk attendants told me to grab my pager and go to the conference room. I was given no other information, but it seemed serious. I closed up shop and made my way to the office, feeling like a kid being called to the principal's office.

When I got there, I saw Max sitting in a swivel chair beside Jamie. Daniel stood at the head of the long table, his face terse. I grabbed a chair on the other side of Max, frowning as I sank into my seat.

"Thanks for being here," Daniel said. His face looked especially pale and I could see grey hairs sprouting at the roots. "We are very grateful to have the two of you here to take care of our ill and injured," he said to Max and me.

"It's no problem," I said automatically without really deciding whether it had been a problem or not. "I'm happy to help."

Daniel slunk down in the chair beside his brother. He looked at the table and took a deep breath to collect his thoughts. I had never seen him so frazzled before.

"This has been a trying time," he said slowly. "We've been unable to have a funeral for my brother because the morgue is running more tests. They can't figure out what killed him. For now, they're calling it a heart attack, but that can't be it. I made it very clear that he was in the best shape of his life. He swam in the ocean every single morning. He wasn't some fat schlep who didn't exercise. He didn't die of a heart attack. He just didn't."

"I agree," I chimed in.

"Good," Daniel said, sounding relieved. "If they

give up, at least I have you to look for the truth. Have you found any leads?"

I wanted to say something about the affair they'd been having with Dawn, but it didn't seem like the right time to bring it up.

"I'm working on it. I've been trying to interview staff and guests when I can."

"Guests," Daniel scoffed. "I'm afraid we won't have many guests this week to talk to."

"Why?" Max asked.

"We've had cancellations, and most of our guests who have been here a while are going home a few days early. We'll still have some guests here, but it's going to look like a ghost town. I have half a mind to just close the place down for a week, but we have to pay our staff. We'd lose a lot of money if we did that. I know that's not really important right now, but if we can't keep this place open, we can't keep all of our staff on board."

"I wouldn't close for the week," I interjected. "There's a good chance that whoever is responsible for all of this is still on the island. If everyone goes home, the investigation will be over."

"And you think it's worth it to continue?" Daniel asked.

I nodded. "I think so."

Daniel pursed his lips. "Then you should do that. I also wanted to let you know that if you choose to stay here, you'll likely be here for another week. When the storm hits, all transportation is cut off. Of course, we want you to have choices here. If you want to leave, you can find a spot on one of the boats leaving the island today. But if you leave, we won't have a medic. I wanted to ask both of you if you would do us the favor of staying on with us. We don't want another incident, and we're afraid we're putting our staff and guests at risk if we don't have someone trained to take care of medical issues."

"I'm going nowhere," Max said.

"I'll stay too," I added. "I don't plan on leaving without providing some closure to this case."

"Good," Daniel said. "I know it's a job for you, but it's very personal for us."

Jamie nodded in agreement. He had been quiet the whole meeting, occasionally sipping from a glass of ice water. I wondered if the constant boozing was taking a toll on his health.

"Again, I'm very sorry for your loss," I said tactfully. "Is it okay if we find a time to chat in the next few days? I'm trying to work on motives for the deaths."

"Of course," Daniel said.

"Sure," Jamie added.

"In the meantime, I recommend you place security cameras around the kitchen," I said. "I have a feeling that whoever is doing the poisoning is using food to do it. Make a big show of placing cameras in the kitchen, bars, and restaurants. That might be enough to deter the suspect."

Daniel nodded. "Consider it done. Now, I need to have a word with the sheriff's office."

"What's the official cause of death?" I asked.

"Accidental death," he said glumly. "The girl was plastered. She got too close to the edge and lost her balance. Now, I just have to assure the police that we're setting up precautions so this doesn't happen again. And I'm going to have to make a donation to the department to thank them for their help, or I'm afraid they're going to take our liquor license. A heavy police presence is the last thing this business needs right now. I'll try to find time to speak with you later," he said. "I don't really know why anyone would want to kill Sebastian, but I'll tell you anything you want to know."

Daniel rushed out of the conference room, closing the door behind him. Jamie got up from his seat and stretched, rubbing his furrowed forehead.

"I can give you something for that headache if you come up to the medical office," I offered to Jamie.

"Thanks, but I'm fine. It's nothing that can't be fixed with a hard workout and a greasy meal. I'll catch up with you guys later."

Max and I sat in our chairs, both quietly thinking. For a second, I almost forgot he was sitting next to me. With everyone leaving the island, my job was about to get much easier or much harder. I just hoped that the storm would purge the resort of all the innocent people, making it easier to spot the bad egg.

"Carlos has nothing," I said, finally breaking the silence.

"Bummer," he replied flatly. "What did he test for?"

"A whole assortment of things. I asked him to test for a few more when he has time. Unfortunately, he doesn't seem to have a lot of that these days. He also sends his best to you."

Max smiled. "I always liked Carlos."

"I'd like him even more if he could find the toxin in the blood sample," I said, half-joking. "I tried to do some research last night, but the internet was so damn slow that I just gave up."

"Then it's a good thing that half the resort is piling onto boats and heading back home today," he said. "I bet by noon, you'll have the fastest internet we've seen in years. To be honest, I've never seen this place so empty, and it's kind of exciting. Of course, it's not good for business," he said, lowering his voice, "but it gives the place a spooky energy."

I rolled my eyes. "The only thing spooky is that someone is sneaking around her with some sort of poison. Now, do you want to help me do some research?"

"I'd love to," he said. "I'll meet you in your room after lunch."

By the time noon rolled around, I was starving. However, I kept wondering if it was safe to eat. I went to the buffet and exclusively chose items I saw on other diners' plates. I ended up with some fried chicken, French fries, and a banana. I grabbed a bottle of beer from the bar and walked back up to my room.

Max was right about it feeling like a ghost town. Usually, I'd pass groups of rowdy college kids or couples holding hands on my walk to my room, but I only spotted a few people lugging suitcases toward the docks. I wasn't sure which perturbed them more—the impending storm or the mysterious deaths.

"Let's get to it," Max said cheerfully as he burst through my door with a bowl of ice cream and a double whiskey.

"You seem excited," I noted.

"The winds have changed," he announced. "I feel like we're going to crack this case wide open."

"Settle down, Sherlock Holmes," I said sarcastically. "Let's just make a list of every natural poison we can find that fits the symptoms. Then, we can rank them in order of probability. That might make it easier for Carlos to track this thing down."

"You're going to be put on a watch list for searching all these things," Max joked.

"You're probably right," I replied as I opened my laptop and began to search. First, I looked up oleander, only because it was the only poison I knew of.

I scanned the first article I could find and listed the symptoms out loud for Max to write down on the piece of paper.

"Nausea and vomiting," I said. "That checks out. It also causes irregular heartbeat. You can be poisoned just from chewing on a flower or a leaf. Write down 'Oleandrin'. That's the name of the compound."

"It says there that death is possible, but unlikely," Max pointed out.

"Maybe if you just eat the plant. I wonder if it can be intensified in an oil or something."

"Could be. What's next?"

"Wolfsbane. It also causes vomiting and heart irregularities. It's capable of stopping the heart. Doll's Eyes can cause cardiac arrest. If you eat enough Columbine, you'll have gastric upset and death. Do you think our perp is sophisticated enough to develop ricin from plants?"

"No clue," Max said. "I wouldn't count that out just yet."

"We can't forget that there are varieties of toxic

mushrooms too," I added. "It wouldn't be so hard to include them in a dish and have them go unnoticed."

Max finished writing and handed the list back to me. "So, what have we learned?"

"Everything we can grow in a backyard can kill us," I scoffed. "Honestly, I had no idea there were so many toxic plants out there. It's kind of scary when you think about it. How many times have you gone to a restaurant and just stuffed your mouth with whatever they gave you without a second thought?"

"Let's not get paranoid," Max said. "Why don't you send this list to Carlos? I'm sure he can do something useful with it."

I pulled out my phone and took a picture of the list before sending it to him. I hoped he'd have some insight into which were likely and which were too farfetched.

"I think I'm going to head to the bar," Max said, yawning. "Want to join me? We can get our drinks faster now that everyone's gone."

I shook my head. "No, I'm going to see if we can eliminate anything from this list," I said, holding the paper up.

"How do you plan on doing that?" he asked.

"Well, there's an entire building on the premises dedicated to rare and exotic plants. Let's see if we can't identify a few."

Max grinned. "Have fun with your botany. Come find me when you've found something interesting."

"Will do," I replied, taking his challenge. I slathered my exposed arms with sunscreen, threw on a hat, and made my way to the greenhouse. I had a feeling I'd be able to find someone to help me identify these deadly plants.

CHAPTER EIGHTEEN

Before I went to the greenhouse, I swung around to one of the beach bars and grabbed a bucket of beers as a gift for the part-owner of the resort. I knocked twice on the greenhouse door before entering, the bucket in front of me as a peace offering.

"Thought you might want to share some beers," I said innocently to Jamie, who was in the process of spraying leaves with a squirt bottle.

"Awesome," he said thankfully. "It's nice of you to think of me. My parents keep telling me to spend time with Daniel, but he's too busy for his only surviving brother. Nevertheless, it's nice to have someone around who just wants to hang out."

"Anytime," I said, prying off the tops of the bottles.

"How's the investigation going?" he asked after taking a long swig.

"It's going," I said. "Actually, I wanted to look around for some specific plants."

"My plants? Why?" he asked, looking alarmed.

"I think someone poisoned your brother and Dawn using a toxic plant that might not show up on the average toxicology screening. I thought I'd see if any of those toxic plants were here."

He frowned. "I think you have the wrong idea. I don't just carelessly buy plants. A lot of them are given as gifts. All the edible herbs can be found in a special section. The kids and the kitchen staff know they can only harvest from there."

"I'm not blaming you. So, you're aware some of your plants can be dangerous if ingested?"

"Sure." He shrugged. "See the plant with those berries over there?"

"Is that a blackberry bush?" I asked, squinting to see the clusters of dark purple fruit."

"No," he said sharply. "That's exactly why I don't keep it with the other edible plants. If you ate one, you'd probably get a stomachache and the shits. There are lots of plants that shouldn't be touched or eaten. For example, too many grapes could kill a dog. I don't keep it here, but poison ivy is a bitch if you accidentally rub up against some. I heard a story about a guy who went camping and used a leaf as toilet paper. He had to go to the emergency room and have someone rub steroid cream on his butt."

I chuckled. "That sounds unpleasant."

"I agree. That's why I don't want anyone ever making that mistake. Most people grow plants that are toxic to people or animals in their yards, or they bring them into their homes. You know the poinsettia every mom and grandma decorates with at Christmas? If a little kid eats enough of one, it's going to ruin Christmas. Or, if you decide to start munching on the lilies in the garden, you're going to be very ill. But I think it's safe to say that most adults don't go around putting leaves into their mouths unless it's something obviously edible and tasty, like mint or basil."

"Yeah, but what if someone is intentionally putting toxic plants in food?" I asked.

He put up his hands defensively. "I'm in here a lot. Most of the time, this place is locked up. I don't know how anyone would even get in here to take something poisonous."

"I'm not accusing you," I said gently. "Do you think you could look over this list and tell me if you have any of these plants?"

He took the list from me and scanned it. "Yeah, I'm pretty sure I have Columbine. I might have some of these others, but a lot of times, there are a lot of common names for plants. I'd have to see the scientific names. Oh, and I don't have any mushrooms here."

He folded the list and handed it back to me.

"Thanks for checking," I said. "The more I can narrow things down, the easier it will be for my friend to check for the poisons."

"What if it came from outside the island?" he asked, finishing his beer.

"That's a possibility."

"What if someone's been taking all the seeds out of the apples? They have trace amounts of cyanide in them, don't they?"

I shook my head. "He tested for cyanide. That wasn't it."

"Oh," he said, his face falling. "I really don't think it came from here. I would have noticed if someone pulled a bunch of flowers off my plants, right?"

I shrugged. I didn't want to mention how drunk he had been in the past few nights. I knew he was hurting from the loss of his brother.

"In fact, let me show you how careful I am with my dangerous specimens," he said, leading me to a glass cabinet far away from the other plants. "This is a manchineel tree. It produces these pretty little fruits. Pretty much every part of this tree will make you super sick. I keep it in glass because just getting too close to it can provide ill effects."

"What happens if you eat it?" I asked, feeling my stomach tighten.

"Oh, your mouth will swell and fill with blisters," he said matter-of-factly. "You might not die, but you're going to be in a world of hurt."

"Oh," I said, mentally crossing it off the list. "Can I ask you why you have something so dangerous you can't even touch it? Where do you even get such a thing?"

He smiled. "They're native to Florida. They're endangered, so someone gave me one as a means to keep them alive. They don't make a lot of sense. Trees need to spread their seeds to reproduce. Most do this by producing yummy fruits for animals to eat. Then, they poop out the seeds, causing a new tree to sprout. These trees don't do that."

"Maybe it's best if they go extinct," I muttered.

"Don't tell that to a scientist," he warned. "I don't disagree that they're not meant for populated areas, but I'm not eager to see any plant go completely extinct."

"Well, it seems like you have things under wraps," I said. When he looked away, I added this note into my collection. Jamie kept poisonous plants but kept them all to himself.

"Jamie" a little voice called out.

"Over here," he responded as he settled down into his lawn chair beside the bucket of beers. He pulled another one out and started sipping on it. I followed suit.

"Hi, Max's friend," Toby said.

I laughed. "You can call me John."

"Where's your sister?" Jamie asked, ruffling the boy's short hair.

"She is reading her book. She says she will come when she is finished," he responded.

"Good kids." Jamie smiled.

"Can I help?" the boy asked.

Jamie looked around, then handed him the spray bottle. "You can finish spraying the plants along that wall. First, tell John why you can't touch the manchineel tree."

Toby crinkled his nose and scowled. "It is a bad tree that makes you very, very sick."

"See?" He winked at the boy. "Even a ten-year-old knows that."

Toby ran toward the parched plants, his sandals flapping on the concrete floor as he went.

"Daniel told the guards to start checking bags a little closer," Jamie said as though it would impress me. "And I bet he'll have those cameras up by the end of the day. I'm really looking forward to finding the asshole who did this to my brother and Dawn—and Amy, for that matter. What are you going to do when you catch the guy?"

I frowned. I hadn't even thought about that part. I was just concerned about not making a total ass of myself.

"Call the police, I guess," I said.

He scoffed. "Why don't you give me a heads-up when you catch him?"

"Why?"

"So I can deliver some justice," he said, his upper lip snarling. "I'm going to make it very easy for the police to arrest this fucker."

"Let's just hold off on the vigilante justice stuff," I said, hoping to deter him from violence. "If we catch this person, the law will handle it. Trust me."

He sighed and took a few long drinks of his beer. He seemed to be calming down a little from his brief outburst.

"Jamie," Toby shouted, running back toward us.

Jamie's demeanor changed instantly. He looked relaxed as the boy zipped in front of us.

"What's up, buddy?" Jamie asked warmly.

"What about that tree over there?" he asked.

"Yeah, go ahead and give it a spray too," he said.

The boy frowned as though he didn't understand what Jamie was saying, but he obeyed and watered the plant.

"I don't mean to sound crazy," Jamie said softly. "I was on the phone with my dad last night. They just want to understand what happened. We all do. Sebastian didn't live a risk-free life, but we didn't expect him to go like this."

"Risky? How so?"

He shrugged and took a drink. "The way a lot of people here take risks. He liked to rock climb and skydive. He partied hard and wasn't afraid to try new things. He wasn't someone who could be held down. That's why he never married. He didn't want to settle. He wanted to swim with the sharks and take hallucinogens in South America. He wanted to screw anyone he wanted. We all accepted him for what he was. He was wild, but I don't think he was reckless. He certainly didn't deserve to die."

"Who would want to hurt him?" I asked.

He shook his head. "That's the thing that Daniel and I keep coming back to. He could be an ass, but he didn't have any serious enemies."

I looked down the aisle between rows of plants to see Toby and Fantine talking closely, almost as if they were arguing. They both wore serious expressions on their faces. Jamie must have noticed that I was looking at them because he called them over.

"Hey, guys," he said. "What's going on?"

Toby grabbed Fantine's hand and started to pull her toward us. She looked worried.

"I tried to tell you," Toby said. "The pong-pong fruits are gone."

Jamie's body went rigid. "What do you mean?"

"I counted them when they were tiny. I counted six fruits on the tree," he said. "Now, there are four."

Jamie's jaw clenched. "Where are the fruits?"

Toby nudged his sister in the side.

"Do you know, Fantine?" he asked gently.

She nodded, her brown eyes going wide. Her lip quivered. "Miss Amy took the fruits. I told her they were bad. She told me that it was okay."

"Why didn't you stop her?" Jamie asked, his voice rising slightly.

"She told me it was okay," Fantine repeated, looking as though she was about to cry.

"Come here," Jamie said, pulling her into his arms. "I know you were only listening to an adult. Sometimes, that is good. You didn't do anything wrong. I just wish you would have told me sooner."

"She said—" Fantine started.

"I know, I know," Jamie said reassuringly. "You knew they were dangerous and you tried to tell her. She didn't listen. You were right and she was wrong. Thank you for telling me now," he said, giving her a hug.

As her face lay buried in his chest, he gave me a dark look. I started to get up from my chair.

"John and I are going to talk to Uncle Daniel," Jamie said to the kids. "I'm going to lock up the greenhouse. I want you two to go to the front office and get an ice cream bar from the staff lounge. Then, you can go to your room and watch cartoons. I'll come by later and take you swimming, okay?"

"Okay," they repeated before running toward the door. Once they were out of sight, Jamie sprung from his chair and marched toward the infamous pong-pong tree. He examined it closely before stomping his foot on the ground.

"That bitch," he roared. "Come look."

I glanced up at where he as pointing. I didn't know much about trees, but I could see what looked like a dried flower with a short stem below it. What I did know was that there were signs plastered to both the container and the tree, warning of its toxicity. You really couldn't miss them.

"She's dead," I thought out loud.

"Good," Jamie growled.

"Not good," I said. "Now, we might never know why she took the fruits from the tree. There will never be closure. Is this the kind of justice you were looking for? Why would a new waitress want to kill the medic and your brother?"

Jamie gritted his teeth. "I–I don't know."

"Well, let's try to find that out before we start

drawing any conclusions," I said, trying to work through my shock.

"I need to talk to Daniel. He needs to know what's going on."

"I'll come with you," I said wearily. "How's he going to take this?" I asked, wanting to be prepared.

"I think he'll be relieved it's over," he said.

"And how are you feeling?" I asked.

He pursed his lips and thought for a moment. "I haven't decided quite yet. Give me a moment."

Together, we locked all the doors to the greenhouse then made the walk to Daniel's personal office. I knew I was supposed to feel some relief, but I just couldn't. There were too many loose ends for this case to feel complete.

CHAPTER NINETEEN

"I don't understand," Daniel said as he sat behind his desk, his face completely blank.

"Amy stole the pong-pong fruits from the tree and put the seeds in the food before she served meals to Dawn and Sebastian," Jamie explained again. "She poisoned them."

I sat in a chair across from Daniel and searched the effects of the plant on my phone. "This seems very likely," I said. "This article says that it's commonly used in suicides because it's so deadly. But it makes note that that seeds are extremely bitter-tasting. What did you have to eat the night of Dawn's death?" I asked.

Daniel opened a file on his computer and searched the date. "Chicken curry," he responded.

"Was it spicy?" I asked.

"Yeah," Jamie answered. "Dawn liked spicy foods.

I think she had the kitchen add extra spice to hers. Sometimes, the kitchen will add certain flavors, given our preferences."

"It's what makes our dining experience special for the guests," Daniel said, trying to follow along. "What did we eat on the night—"

"Jambalaya," I answered before he could finish the question. "It was so spicy, I could hardly eat it. It's the spice that covers up the bitterness. I suppose you could put the seeds in anything with a very strong flavor—like coffee or really sweet desserts."

"Shit," Daniel swore. "We can't keep the kitchen open. It's too dangerous. We don't know if anyone else was involved. We don't know if the seeds were used in anything else."

"Well, there's no one here," Jamie said dryly. "We could eat nothing but Twinkies if we wanted to."

"It's our responsibility to take care of our guests and our staff," Daniel said sternly. "What if this continues to happen?"

"Will it?" Jamie asked. "It seems pretty certain that it begins and ends with Amy."

I bit my lip. "I don't mean to pry, but do you know anything about a relationship between your brother and the waitress? How about your brother and Dawn? I know this is getting very personal, but I need to know what's going on if I can piece this together. I wouldn't ask unless it was very important."

Daniel and Jamie exchanged a glance. I could tell they were wordlessly coming to an agreement right before my eyes.

"Sebastian had relations with Dawn," Daniel said flatly.

"Sexual relations? How often?"

"Fairly regularly," Daniel said after pausing to think.

"Was he having relations with anyone else?"

Jamie snorted, as though he was recalling a fond memory of his late brother. "Only anything that moved."

"Can you provide me with anything more specific?"

The brothers exchanged a glance again.

"Mostly guests," Daniel said. "I didn't much care for his picking them out of the herd that way. God forbid he knocks a few up and he has to worry about that for the rest of his life. That, and I was always concerned that they would be a little too drunk for him. Luckily, we never had an incident."

"Would you say you knew all of your brother's partners?" I asked.

Jamie looked at the floor and wrung his hands in his lap.

"No," Daniel answered, "but he wasn't sneaky about it. Even if he'd tried to be discreet, someone would find out. There are eyes and ears everywhere."

"He was fucking my wife," Jamie said, not making eye contact with either of us. "I think she might have been in love with him."

I quickly changed the subject. "What about Amy? Had he ever been seen with her?"

Daniel shook his head. "I don't think so. Did someone tell you they were together?"

"No," I replied, "but if they were, we have a motive."

I had worked this through my mind a few times. Amy was young and inexperienced. She met Sebastian and he seduced her. One of the resort owners wanted to be with her, and it could potentially be huge for her career if things went well. They slept together, perhaps a few times, and she was smitten. After all, he was rich, handsome, and charming.

However, one night, she might have gone to visit Sebastian, only to find him humping Dawn. After all, it seemed like a regular occurrence. Amy was hurt by this. She stalked Sebastian, still hoping that he'd leave the medic and go back to her. Instead, he found him cheating with Cara. This was the final straw.

Amy harvested the fruit of the deadly pong-pong tree while Jamie wasn't around. The kids sneaked up on her, but she told them to mind their own business. Obedience and respect for authority were engrained in those kids' brains before they could even talk. Poor Fantine stepped back as Amy stripped the poison from the tree, harvesting the seeds for her revenge.

Dawn was an easy target. She didn't know that anyone wanted to hurt her. The free-spirited woman loved everyone, and everyone loved her in return—except Amy. On a night where the spicy curry flavors covered the bitter seed, Amy garnished the meal with the toxin. Dawn, assuming she had a case of food poisoning, went to her room to rest. Her body was found some time later.

After the first killing, Amy's anger had not subsided. She wanted to purge the island of everyone who'd had a hand in her pain. Sebastian was next. She waited until another spicy meal was featured and served him a plate of poison. Cara might have fallen to the poison that night as well, but her meal came from a separate batch. Perhaps Amy had made a mistake.

Feeling guilty and depressed about killing her lover, Amy took to the booze. An inexperienced drinker, she went too hard, getting herself blind drunk in the middle of the day. If she showed up to work, she would be fired. She had been saving up to send money back home. If she returned emptyhanded, her family would be so disappointed. She had nothing left.

In deep despair, she walked too close to the cliff. When her foot slipped, she didn't correct her balance. Instead, she felt the relief of the finished fight as she plunged onto the sandy beach below. She had her revenge. There was nothing left for her now.

I sat in Daniel's office, practically in a trance as I went over my latest theory. I didn't have solid evidence to back a few parts up, but at least all the pieces fit together. Now, if I could get some confirmation that Amy and Sebastian were sleeping together, then I would feel confident enough to call it a day.

"I think I need to talk to the kitchen staff again," I announced, standing up from my chair.

"I'll go with you," Jamie said.

"Me too," Daniel added. "We need answers."

On the way into the kitchen, I saw one of the waitresses I spoke to the previous day. I gestured to her and brought her to a quiet corner of the outdoor dining area.

"Can I ask you something?" I asked, dropping my voice.

"Sure." She giggled nervously.

I bit my lip, trying to find the right words for my query without sounding like a pervert and causing more rumors to spread. In the end, I just got down to it.

"I have a question about Amy. Do you know if she was . . . dating anyone?"

She thought for a moment, then shook her head with confidence. "No, I don't think so. I remember her talking about her parents and younger siblings, but she never mentioned a boyfriend. Besides, it's hard to be in a relationship with people outside of the island. I really doubt she was dating anyone."

I took a deep breath. "I guess what I'm really asking is, was she intimate with anyone on the island?"

The girl took a moment to process my question and then let out a shrill giggle. "Oh, my goodness, no. I'm quite confident Amy was a virgin. Like, she would get so uncomfortable when we'd have tables of honeymooners practically groping each other. In fact, I used to laugh about it with the other girls. She never joined in when we talked about the hot guys and girls at our tables. She was so young too. I'd be shocked if she had even kissed a guy, the way she acted about that stuff."

"Okay, thanks," I said awkwardly, rejoining the brothers. I felt strangely disappointed by the answer. I wasn't about to completely disregard my theory, but it certainly didn't help how Amy looked as a suspect.

I returned to the brothers, unable to hide my disappointment. "Let's talk to George," I said. "He seemed to know her a little better than the others. I don't know if he would know this particular detail about Amy, but he might have some information."

The brothers followed me into the kitchen, where

we found George labeling prep containers in the back. I was about to call out to him when Jamie reached out and grabbed my arm.

"Look," he said, pointing to the trashcan beside me.

I frowned. I didn't see anything but food waste. Carrot peels covered watermelon rinds, speckled with coffee grounds.

"That," he said sharply, pointing to the peel of a small fruit. "That's from the pong-pong tree. That's my fruit. That's what killed my brother."

"Crap," I hissed under my breath. The remains of the fruit sat near the top of the pile. This was placed in there recently.

"Everybody, stop what you're doing," Daniel bellowed, surprising me with his raised voice. Everyone else must have been shocked, too, because the bustling kitchen went completely silent.

"What's going on?" George asked, waddling over to us.

"We have reason to believe that some food has been tainted. Until we know what's safe, we need to halt our food service."

"We can't do that," George cried. "Dinner is only a few hours away."

"People could die," Daniel emphasized. "Until we know it's safe, we cannot serve."

"My kitchen is clean," George argued. "There's no threat of food poisoning here."

I pointed to the trash. "Have you been cooking with this particular fruit?" I asked.

He frowned. "Yes. I had Amy get it from the greenhouse a few days ago. I was under strict instructions to only use it when specially ordered."

I rubbed at my forehead. "George, it's extremely toxic. We think this was what was used to kill Dawn and Sebastian."

"No," he said in disbelief. "I was told that it could be dangerous if it wasn't prepared in the right way, but we washed the fruit off the seeds. That's the dangerous part. And I know that it's super expensive, so I can only use it on special dishes. I didn't even try any."

"Good, because if you did, you'd be dead," I said, trying to wrap my head around his ignorance. "Was Amy involved in this besides fetching the fruits?"

He shook his head as he struggled to understand what was going on. "No. I would have gotten it myself, but I was too busy so I sent her to get the ingredients."

My leading theory was officially bunk. Amy wasn't having an affair with Sebastian. She was just an innocent woman in the wrong place at the wrong time. She didn't kill anyone—she was just an accidental accomplice.

"George," I said gently, yet firmly. "Who ordered

the pong-pong seed? It's very important that we hear the entire story."

It was in this moment that he realized that he was in deep trouble. "Let me get my planner," he said slowly. He walked to the back office and closed the door behind him.

"What is happening?" Jamie moaned. "This is insanity. Someone put the hit out on my brother and our head chef is so dumb that he just takes orders from anyone. I don't care if he's innocent. I think we should fire him."

"Let's wait until we hear what he has to say," Daniel said anxiously. "We don't want to scare him off."

I looked out among the kitchen staff to find that they were all silently staring at us. I looked over at Daniel.

He cleared his throat. "I don't want any of you to be alarmed, but some of your food might be contaminated. A poisonous plant was brought in and potentially used to cause harm to some of our staff. I'm sorry, but if there are any leftovers in the refrigerator, they must be thrown out. We'll have George start on a new menu, but unfortunately, we could have a huge liability on our hands. I appreciate your hard work, and believe me, you will be compensated for this extra work."

I heard a lot of mutters and sighs as the prep chefs

took to the refrigerator and started tossing food into the trash.

"What's taking him so long?" Jamie said, standing on the balls of his feet. "I don't think we need to see his planner for proof. I just need him to tell me who ordered the pong-pong."

"I'll check on him," I said, fearing that he might have evidence that he was trying to get rid of. I opened the door to his office and found that there was another door leading to the outside.

"He's gone," I said to the brothers. My stomach dropped, fearing that he was going to take his secrets to the grave. "He made a run for it."

"I'm going to find him," Jamie said with determination, sprinting out of the kitchen before acknowledging either of us.

"I'm going to call security," Daniel said, reaching for his phone. "He's not going to get off this island without going through us."

"I need to make a phone call," I said abruptly. "I'll catch up with you guys soon."

CHAPTER TWENTY

"Carlos!" I panted into the phone. Sweat was dripping down my face after my run to my room. "I think I have the answer."

"You cracked the case?" he asked. "Congrats, John Boy."

"Not yet," I wheezed. "I think I've pinpointed the toxin. It's pong-pong seed."

"Huh?" he asked. I was expecting him to be more familiar with the toxin.

"It's some sort of weird, rare tree. Can you look in your databases and find some information on it for me? There's a chance that people are still at risk, so I'd like to find some sort of antidote, if possible."

"Yeah, give me a second," he said. I heard the sound of typing keys in the background. "You caught me at a good time. I'm just finishing up a few dictations before lunch. Okay, I've found your toxin. I can't believe I've never heard of this before."

"What does it say?" I asked eagerly.

"Here's a case where a woman ordered the seeds online a few years ago. She was trying to commit suicide. It doesn't seem like a very pleasant method. It seems like she was in some pain."

"Did she survive?" I asked.

Carlos muttered to himself as he skimmed the article. "Yeah, someone found her shortly after she ingested the seeds. Luckily, the name of the plant was stamped on the envelope and the emergency room she went to happened to know what to give her. Good for them—it looks like they saved her life at the last moment. She later went on to make a full recovery."

"Wow," I said, feeling relieved that there was some sort of cure. "What did they give her?"

"Let's see," he said. He typed something into his computer. "It appears that there's a pretty good poison antagonist out there." He chuckled. "And wouldn't you know, it's also used for oleander poisoning. Yep, it says that Digibind is effective for oleandrin and digitalis poisoning. You were on the right track."

"Not exactly," I said, downplaying my hunch. "Oleander doesn't even grow here. If some kids hadn't noticed the poisonous fruits were missing, I would have never guessed what it was."

"Me neither," he said. "It says that this particular toxin is almost impossible to find in an autopsy. It's just so rare that no one would think to look for it. I'll still test your sample for it, but if you have good reason to believe that's what killed them, then I'm sure you're right. No well-meaning medical examiner would have found it without a tip from an investigator. The cause of death would have been written off as cardiac arrest every time."

I half-smiled. It wouldn't change anything about the deaths, but at least it might provide an ounce of closure to the families of the deceased. I still needed to figure out who was the mastermind behind it. My next suspect would be George, but there was nothing masterful about that mind.

"It also says that the seeds are bitter, so—"

"It's often found in very sweet or very spicy food," I finished. "Yeah, we figured that part out. So, is there anything you can have sent over here?"

There was silence on the other end. For a second, I thought we had lost the connection.

"I'm not sure about the logistics of that."

"You see my concern, though," I said quickly. "This could happen again. I want to be prepared if someone shows up to my office again on the brink of death."

"You could send them to the ER with direct orders to administer the Digibind."

"That's not going to work," I said. "By the time we got Sebastian shipped out, it was already too late. I need something that works faster. I need a few bottles of solution. If no boats or helicopters are clear to come here, then staying here is basically a death sentence if the poison is ingested. I'm working with an active homicide case here."

He cleared his throat. "You'd have to administer quite a bit of it to reverse the toxicity. Besides, you're not a practicing physician. I don't know how you're going to get large quantities of a drug from a manufacturer."

"Can't you just write me a prescription and have it delivered here by courier?" I pleaded. "There's a storm coming. We might not get another chance."

"I don't know." He groaned. "It doesn't seem ethical or legal."

"Let me deal with any fallout," I said desperately. "If anyone asks, I just stole it from you or lied to get the prescription. Please, I wouldn't be asking like this unless it was absolutely necessary."

He sighed loudly. "When do you need it by? Can I have someone ship it out at the end of the day?"

I bit my lip. "I don't know if the boat would make it before the storm. Do you think there's any way we can get it here sooner? The resort will pay for all the expenses."

"Let me see what I can do," he said, sounding stressed. "How soon can you have a boat to the docks?"

I looked out my window at people dragging roller suitcases to the boats.

"Probably in an hour or so. They're basically running a ferry service right now, but that's going to stop once the storm rolls in. I can send you the information for the courier. You can address the package directly to me and maybe make note that it's for the medical office. People will just think it's a shipment of our normal medical supplies. Do you think you can make this happen?"

Another long pause. I was afraid he was going to find a way to let me down easy.

"Yeah, I think I can hook you up. Give me some time to find the stuff. I'll keep you updated."

I grinned broadly. "You're the man, Carlos," I said.

"Save your ass-kissing for when it actually arrives," he said.

I hung up the phone feeling a little bit lighter. If the antagonist came through, then we had a chance of saving the next victim's life. With that taken care of, I needed to find the other brothers and make sure that the delivery would come through without a hitch.

With my recent discovery about Amy, it was back to the drawing board. I could say with some certainty that George was involved to some degree, though I hadn't thought of him as a suspect until the moment he disappeared. I worked through all the information in my notebook, searching for a motive for George to kill.

Just from spending some time with him, I got the feeling that the man pined after women he could never have. He was smitten with Cara Bergeron, despite the fact that she was married and way out of his league. He'd also mentioned how pretty Amy was, though she was thirty years his junior. I had seen the way he looked at other beautiful women in the dining room. He was the type of guy who desperately wanted some tail but could never get it.

He was a nice enough guy, but it was clear as to why he'd never had a chance with any of these women. He was pudgy, balding, and not conventionally attractive in any way. When he opened his mouth, it was clear that he wasn't highly educated or cultured. He knew his stuff when it came to cuisine and ran a good kitchen, but he wasn't the envy of the resort. This place was filled with people looking to score with other hotties. No one came here to hook up with a tubby chef.

From what I could tell, there was nothing sinister to George. He wasn't creepy toward the women but was the type to be fooled by flirting and sweet talk. I never got the impression that he wanted to hurt anyone.

First, I thought about George's relationship with Dawn. Dawn had a reputation for sleeping around, so I would have to ask around again to see if they were ever together. My guess was that the young and vibrant Dawn was more interested in people her age, though I couldn't know for sure.

He seemed to be upset about both of the poisonings, though that wasn't always a reliable form of information. People grieved in different ways. Just like someone who showed no emotions could be innocent, someone who showed too many could be guilty.

As far as I could tell, George didn't have a problem with Sebastian either. I had seen them chatting and it appeared as if they were pals. All the Bergeron brothers seemed to have a good relationship with their chef.

Then, there was Amy. George told me firsthand that she was one of his favorite waitresses. Unless I had misjudged his character, there was no reason for him to want to harm her. In fact, there didn't seem like there was any reason for anyone to harm her. The only thing she was guilty of was being tricked into harvesting a poisonous fruit used to kill two staff members.

Unless George had been experiencing bouts of psychosis, there was no reason for him to kill. The only theory I could scrape together was a scenario where he had been rejected by too many women and went into a jealous rage. Perhaps he killed Dawn because she apparently slept with every man at the resort except for him. Then, he killed Sebastian because he was everything that George wasn't. Then, he killed poor Amy because she was the only other witness to his crimes. Once the authorities traced the poison source, she would know of her role and would admit her part in the plot, effectively outing him.

It was a stretch, but if I could procure some evidence to support it, it might just hold up. Now, we just had to find the man so we could give him a proper interview, now that I knew what questions to ask.

From my experience as a private investigator, I knew that running away never looked good for a suspect. I'd chased enough people to know that running away was a terrible option when trying to establish innocence. The bail skippers that I caught all happened to receive guilty verdicts. That didn't seem like a coincidence.

"Damn it, George," I muttered. "I trusted you."

I was realizing that I'd let first impressions get the best of me. In every interaction with George, I thought he seemed like a trustworthy and helpful guy. Now, I knew he was hiding something about the murders. I just wondered how many other potential subjects I had been wrong about.

I heard pounding on my door, which nearly caused

my heart to leap out of my chest. I raced to open it and found Daniel, standing with his hands on his hips.

"Did you find him?" I asked, my heart still racing.

"Not yet," he said. "I've decided I'm going to go on the search. I want you to come with me."

"Why me?" I asked.

He pursed his lips together and looked nervous. "Max tells me you're skilled in hand to hand combat."

"I'm okay," I said, wondering what other tall tales about me were floating around.

"Well, I'm not. I'm not walking around that jungle by myself while a murderer is on the loose."

"Right," I said, suddenly feeling nervous. "Before we go, can I ask you a favor?"

"What?" he asked impatiently.

"I just ordered some necessary medical supplies for the office. Can I make sure that they're delivered to my office without anyone tampering with them?"

"Yeah, just tell the front office what you need," he said. "We'll pass them on the way to the jungle. Are you ready to go now?"

I eyed my bottle of sunscreen on the TV stand. I didn't think that Daniel had the patience for my careful application of sunblock, so I just grabbed my cap.

"Ready," I said.

"Good," he said tersely. "This might take a while."

CHAPTER TWENTY-ONE

I practically had to run to keep up with Daniel. He took long, brisk strides toward the edge of the resort's boundary. By the time we got to the barrier, my T-shirt was sticking to my back with sweat, and we still had farther to go.

"Do you own the whole island?" I asked.

He nodded, his eyes locked straight ahead. "We bought the real estate during the financial crisis. The previous owner was a big shot in the recording industry, but he lost everything and had to sell it. Since he was desperate, we got it at a reasonable cost. It was a little more land than we needed to start the resort, but it gave us room for growth."

Daniel punched a five-digit code into the gate, allowing us to pass the barrier into the wilderness. Immediately, I was struck with the thick humidity of the air. Tiny bugs swarmed in front of my face. It was as if we had completely departed the island.

"Does everyone have the gate code?" I asked.

"No. There are ways to get into the jungle. We only created a visible wall to deter people from doing their own exploration."

"Is there anything dangerous in here?" I asked nervously.

"You'll find some snakes and a bunch of mosquitoes, but nothing deadly. Although, now that I know my brother keeps poisonous plants on the premises, I can't say for certain that there are none growing out here. No, the biggest reason we block it off is because we don't want to spend the money to hire security to make sure no one gets lost out there."

That made me feel a little better. I'd experienced the swamps of Florida, but I was still wary of the unknown in the dense bush. Now, the biggest threat was a portly chef on the run.

"We were planning on adding more luxury cabins out here one day," Daniel said as we walked between trees and bushes. "Right now, the only ones we have are for the owners. I don't know what we're going to do with Sebastian's. It doesn't feel right renting it out."

"Do you think you'll live on the island forever?" I asked.

He shrugged. "Why not? I don't have a lot else. I

just hope that this isn't the end of our dream."

We walked in silence for a while. I felt uncomfortable pressing for personal information at such a vulnerable time, but I needed answers.

"Does it seem reasonable to assume that George might have had a sexual relationship with Dawn? I've heard some unsubstantiated rumors, but it might lead to a motive."

He scoffed. "No. There's just no way."

"Why do you say that?"

He gritted his teeth. "I . . . I know her preferences."

"Any greater insight?"

He exhaled loudly. "I know because I've had a sexual relationship with her."

I raised my eyebrows. "Both you and your brother?"

"And Jamie."

I tried not to show any judgment or emotion at this response. I just wanted him to keep talking to me.

"That's got to be a little messy, right? I mean, I was cheated on and it didn't feel good to see my girl in bed with another guy. This doesn't take sibling rivalry to a whole other level?"

Daniel looked straight ahead as we walked. I couldn't imagine how three brothers could share one woman and not want to kill one another. It would be the perfect motive.

"Actually, we got along just fine."

Now I was curious. "If you don't mind my asking—how?"

A faint smile came to his lips. "I suppose my parents taught us how to share from a young age. I suppose we each had our moments of jealousy, but we worked through it. Dawn was more than just a good time, though. She was our friend and an incredible asset to our resort. I think each of us got something different from her. To me, she was a great companion when I got lonesome. To Sebastian, she was the sexual outlet he craved. To Jamie, Dawn was a caring woman who gave him affection without demanding more out of him."

I might have felt envy toward men like the Bergeron brothers in the past, but I could see that being rich and handsome wasn't enough to be happy. Each brother had their own tragic story that I was uncovering as I asked questions.

Daniel was the stereotypical workaholic. While his brothers had fun, he kept the family business thriving by never taking a day off resort operations, even when his brother died. He was no-nonsense by nature and had assumed total responsibility for the resort, for better or worse. His life revolved around his job, so much so that he'd never allowed himself to settle down with a woman. It wasn't as though it would be hard if he applied himself—on the outside, he appeared to have it all. But at forty-one, it was getting harder for him to court potential suitors. It had been so long since he had tried. Instead of creating a fulfilling relationship with someone, he had Dawn, a proxy for the physical relationship he needed.

On the surface, Jamie also seemed to have it all. He was in the prime of his life but absolutely miserable. He had the potential to get everything he wanted out of life, but he couldn't get it for some reason. I could tell that he had aspirations of becoming a Coach Dad, carting kids to their soccer or baseball games, shouting calls and encouragement from the sideline. I'd seen his temper flare, but he was such a natural with the twins, so patient and calm, even in the midst of disaster. But as long as he stayed with Cara, he would never have them. I wondered if she had been a different person when they'd married. She was still beautiful, but everyone could tell that there was little love in that marriage. I still didn't understand cheating on a partner, but in his situation, maybe I'd come to terms with why he needed a lover who didn't cause emotional anguish. Dawn softened the edges that the alcohol couldn't touch.

But would either of their incomplete lives cause them to kill? The more I thought about it, the more absurd it seemed that three brothers could share a lover and not experience any negative results.

"But isn't it weird?" I pressed, trying to get the answer I was looking for. "I mean, I wouldn't want to think about any of my siblings having sex, but it's got to be hard to ignore when you're with the same woman."

He gave me a funny look. "Somehow, I managed. I really didn't think about that. I was more focused on her."

"Right," I said, feeling like a creep. "But you know that she had other lovers?"

"Sure." He shrugged as if it was a silly thing to say. "There were staff members and the occasional guest when she wasn't on duty. But she was careful, and so was I. She knew how to keep herself safe."

I knew he was talking about undesired consequences of sex, but I couldn't help but spot the irony in his statement. Why would someone kill her?

"But I can assure you, she never slept with George. My brothers and I devised a system where we would not seek her out on the same day, and we limited ourselves to two days with her so we wouldn't feel jealous if she was spending more time with one of us than another."

I stifled a giggle. "It sounds like you guys mastered polygamy."

He didn't seem to like this remark. "It's best not to

put labels on things. If you don't call it a relationship, you can't get hurt if it ends."

I wasn't sure I was following his logic, but I understood what he meant. He had really committed himself to closing off all emotions.

"So what makes you so sure she was never with George? Just the mere fact that there weren't enough hours in the day?"

"Actually, yes. But also, she was way out of his league. I know you didn't know her, but she was very pretty and smart."

"That's not really proof that there was never a relationship," I said.

"You're just going to have to take my word for it. Would you have sex with just anyone? Even if the girl was really unfortunate looking, old, and a little awkward?"

"No," I said, crinkling up my nose. "But I'm not that desperate."

"And neither was she," he concluded. "I understand that a girl gets a reputation for the lovers she takes, but she was more than that reputation. Just because she shared a unique relationship with a few people, it doesn't mean that she was just giving herself away to everyone. Besides, I've never really heard George express feelings for her."

"He said that she was a good woman," I said,

recalling our conversation.

"That is accurate."

"Did you love her?" I asked, taking a long shot.

He exhaled sharply through his nose. "Not in a romantic way, no. I loved her as a friend. I never had the chance to mourn her loss because my brother's came so quickly after. Now, I feel myself mourning for a waitress I had only seen in passing, though she was the one who delivered the poison fruit. Excuse me for saying this, but I'm not sure you're asking the right questions."

I felt like I had been punched in the stomach. All along, I'd feared that I would be found out as a phony, a glorified bounty hunter trying to solve a triple-homicide.

"What should I be asking?" I asked, my voice wavering.

"Well, when we find him, you can ask George why he fled and why he ordered Amy to retrieve the poison in the first place."

I bit my tongue. While I absolutely planned on doing so if we caught George, I didn't want to let Daniel know that he and his brother were still suspects in this investigation. I just couldn't rule any connected party out until I had some solid evidence.

A thought I hadn't previously considered came to mind. All along, I figured George was guilty because he ran. But it was possible that he only ran out of fear of consequences for spilling the beans. Perhaps he was sworn to secrecy, and if he made mention about the original food request, he would be killed, just like the others.

Sensing that Daniel was on the verge of being offended by my prying questions, I quickly changed the subject to something easier to talk about—his work. I didn't want to talk him into a place that would ultimately cause him to close off from me.

"So, what are you going to do about the food?" I asked.

He relaxed, his mind comfortable with business on the forefront, even though it was a stressful situation.

"We've got to switch to completely bland things with mostly fresh ingredients. We'll be serving lots of packaged goods and fresh fruits and vegetables. Luckily, we mostly have to worry about feeding the staff, who won't leave us bad reviews for a lack of hot food. The assistant kitchen manager is working on salads and sandwiches right now, and we've sent out a company-wide memo to stop eating if anyone tastes something bitter in their food. I know it's not much, but it's the best we can do."

I nodded reassuringly. "That's good. Maybe it will be enough of a deterrent that if there are any more seeds left, the perp will give up."

"That's what I'm hoping. Unfortunately, we're bound to run out of packaged food sometime, and I just hope that the storm passes soon so we can get a new shipment. If we ever get new guests again, it's vital that this issue is taken care of."

Basically, Daniel was letting me know that if his business failed, it was because I was unable to catch the person poisoning the employees. The pressure must have motivated me, because I found myself leading the way as we searched the jungle together, looking for the runaway chef.

Eventually, we had to call off our search. The sun was about to set, and we had no source of light on our person. It was the last place I wanted to be with a murderer on the loose.

Feeling a little discouraged, Daniel and I parted ways at the front office. He went into his private study and I went to the medical office. After handing out ibuprofen to a landscaper with a headache, I opened a large box on the counter, addressed to me.

Inside, I found more boxes filled with bottles of the poison antagonist. I felt like a child on Christmas morning, beaming as I opened the parcel. Now, if anyone suffered from mysterious symptoms, it wouldn't be a death sentence.

I thought about telling Daniel about this good news, but I hesitated to pick up the phone. For the most part, I trusted Daniel, but I wasn't on the island to make friends. Even though he was paying me, I couldn't completely assume that he had nothing to do with the deaths—not yet, anyway. I needed to remain impartial, find the real killer, and save lives in the process. If word got out that I had the antidote, the killer may have to resort to sneakier methods—ones that I might not be able to reverse. I wanted the killer to think that their mode was completely foolproof and that I was completely helpless.

I whispered a word of thanks to Carlos after reading the dosage instructions. Then, before anyone knew I had it, I stored the medication. Moving rolls of paper towels and boxes of tissues aside, I pushed the medication toward the back and carefully covered it back up with the innocuous items.

I was excited to have the medication at my disposal if an emergency called for it. However, I realized that my excitement to see if it worked was a little macabre. Of course, it would be ideal if I didn't need to use it. And with all the new precautions going into place, it would be much harder to poison food. Still, I had a nagging suspicion that the perp would need to be caught in the act, which meant that some poor person's health would be sacrificed in the process. I just hoped I could deliver the antidote in time.

CHAPTER TWENTY-TWO

Not long after I returned to the medical office, the storm began to stir. The palm trees swayed ominously as dark clouds covered the blinding sun. Though I knew the rain would soon fall, I couldn't help but feel thankful for the change in weather. My skin was on its way to becoming brighter than my ginger hair.

If there was any sign of liveliness before the storm hit, it was gone now. The majority of the guests had fled for sturdier ground, leaving employees without a job to do. From my window, I watched pool staff carry umbrellas to storage closets, fighting with them as they threatened to unfurl. Housekeeping staff stood in their uniforms, watching the clouds sweep in, their arms folded around their chests as they watched the sky.

Realizing I had missed dinner, I headed to the buffet line for supper. Grabbing tongs, I put a slightly-soggy grilled chicken sandwich on my plate before realizing the only condiments available were ketchup and mayo. Then, I dished up a serving of French fries and snagged a banana before sitting down at a single table. As I ate my bland but not horrible meal, I watched the other employees take their daily rations. For the most part, employees generally ate their meals in a separate space, but with the threat of poison, everyone ate together, under the watchful eyes of the security cameras.

Small-talk about the weather became the primary dinner conversation. Everyone within earshot was either complaining about the storm or giddy because the lack of guests meant more free time. Lifeguards talked excitedly about what they would do while the pools were closed, while people from maintenance fretted about losing power. No one seemed concerned about the mysterious deaths that had been occurring around the little private island. That was already old news, and people seemed more worried about when the good food would return than when George would be found.

After dinner, I returned to the medical office, only to discover that my job was easier with the storm approaching. With fewer guests around, I had fewer people coming in for simple maladies. The only person who came to visit me in the three hours I sat up there was a maintenance worker who had an injured hand from the wind slamming a door shut on it as he was repairing the latch mechanism. I splinted and wrapped it, handed him a few ibuprofen and an ice pack, and sent him on his way. The rest of the time, I lay on the paper-covered exam table and stared up at the lights, watching them flicker as the island started to lose power.

At some point, I must have drifted off to sleep, because the next thing I knew, hushed voices were approaching me. I snapped my eyes open and sat up straight, pretending I had not been sleeping on the job. A nervous front desk worker approached me, a walkie-talkie in hand.

"Something's happened at Jamie Bergeron's cabin," she said worriedly.

"What's happened?" I asked. "A poisoning?"

She shook her head. "No, but your presence is requested. It's urgent."

Without even thinking to grab my bag of supplies, I took off toward the luxury cabins. I sprinted down the concrete ramps, the wind pushing against me as I went. Then, I turned a corner, and the wind was at my back, propelling me toward unknown danger.

I could hear the yelling from about fifty yards

away. When I got to Jamie's cabin, I saw a figure on the ground, being held down by Jamie and a security guard.

"What's going on?" I panted.

"Help me," a faint voice said. In the dim light, I couldn't tell if this person was in danger or if the rest of us were. Then, a few feet back, I saw Cara sitting on the ground, her knees up to her chest. Tears poured down her face as she rubbed her throat. I knelt down to the ground to see a chubby red face sputter as he begged for freedom.

"George," I breathed. "Can someone tell me what's going on?"

"I'll tell you," Jamie snarled. "I was coming back to the cabin to secure the windows for the storm. Cara wasn't home and I wasn't sure where she was. Then, I heard a terrible noise coming from behind the house and saw this asshole strangling my wife."

My mouth gaped open. Upon hearing this brief recap, Cara started howling in pain. I walked over toward her to examine her neck. Meanwhile, more security guards arrived, bound George's wrists with zip ties, and brought him to his feet.

"Where should we put him?" I heard one guard ask.

"Toss him over the side of the cliff like he did to

that waitress," Jamie growled. Cara involuntarily squeaked, her voice raw.

"No," George cried. "I didn't hurt her."

"Shut up," Jamie bellowed. "Take him to the kitchen storage room and make sure the door is locked."

"Make sure he's unharmed and has food and water," I muttered into the ear of a guard as he passed. I wanted to be able to interview him after I finished checking on Cara.

"Should I call the police?" a guard asked Jamie.

"And what would they do?" he retorted. "The sea is impassable and no one is going to fly a helicopter in this weather. He'll have to stay here until we can get rid of him."

The guards frog-marched George to his cell as he struggled and called out to me, muttering all sorts of things about being innocent. I would have time to talk to him later. Now, I had to interview the Bergerons and ensure that Cara was okay. She looked to be in shock, something I couldn't blame her for. I would be shocked if I were attacked out of nowhere.

I lightly traced my fingers down Cara's slim neck, examining her for any extensive damage. Red welts bloomed on her tanned skin. She would be left with nasty bruises around her neck for some time.

"Are you injured anywhere else?" I asked her. She

had light scratches on her face and arms, but other than that, she looked relatively unscathed.

"I hit my head on the ground when he attacked me," she said, lifting a hand to her tousled hair.

I pulled out my little flashlight I had stored in my pocket when the power started to flicker and held it in front of her face. Her pupils shrank and her eyes tracked the light. I couldn't be certain, but I didn't think she had any brain trauma.

"Tell me exactly what happened," I said. Her husband tried to get her off the ground and into a chair, but she wouldn't budge. She still looked terrified.

"I was inside gathering candles," she said, nodding her head toward their living room, just beyond the back door. "I wanted to have them lit in case all the lights went out. I like the soft light during a storm. It feels romantic."

Her voice trailed off and she looked at the ground, away from Jamie.

"Anyway," she continued, "I heard a noise. I was worried about the lawn chairs breaking the windows, so I came out to stack them. That's when hands reached out from nowhere and wrapped around my neck. I think I might have blacked out. I don't exactly remember what happened."

Her hands were shaking. For someone who could be so intimidating to others, she seemed very rattled, perhaps more so than she had been when Sebastian was in my care.

"That's when I got home and called security," Jamie interjected. "I let him have it too."

"I don't blame you," I said, noticing that Jamie was becoming defensive. "Cara, do you have any idea what would have caused him to do this?"

She shook her head quickly. "None."

"He's only ever spoken highly of you," I said.

"You–you've talked about me?" she asked, looking surprised.

I shrugged. "It must have come up in passing. It's not like he spoke ill of you," I said, trying to reassure her. I knew how important appearances were to her. "He told me that you were very kind and a friend."

"We weren't friends," she said quickly. "I don't know him that well. I mean, I have some input when it comes to the dining room decorations and linens and table settings, but we were never close. I think he's in love with me."

"Is that so?" I asked, wondering if George had misunderstood his relationship with Cara. I wasn't completely surprised that they weren't as close as he led on.

"I mean, he tried to kill me," she rasped. "A friend wouldn't do that. I think he was in love with me, but he couldn't have me. Maybe he came here tonight to take advantage of me."

"Oh, my God," Jamie said, sinking down into the chair beside his wife. I winced at the thought of him doing more damage than he'd already done.

"I need to find Daniel," Jamie said firmly. "He needs to know about this."

"Don't go," Cara cried. "Please don't leave me alone. I'm scared."

"No one is going to harm you," Jamie said reassuringly. "I'll have someone stay outside the house if you want."

"I don't feel so good," Cara said, raising her hand to her head. I wasn't sure if that was the fear talking or if she really had something wrong with her that I couldn't detect. Either way, it was best to play it safe.

"I think you should come with me to the medical office," I said. "I can clean up those scratches and give you something to help you relax."

"Yes," she said, her shaky hand finding mine. "Yes, I need something to help me relax."

"Okay," Jamie said, a look of deep concern on his face. "I'll come get you when I'm done talking to Daniel."

"You're not going to talk to George, are you?" she asked.

"Why shouldn't I?" Jamie asked.

"She's probably right," I chimed in. "I should probably be the one to talk to him."

"Fine," Jamie said, grabbing his rain jacket and pulling it on over his shirt. "I'll be back soon," Jamie said, kissing his wife on the head. She winced at his touch.

I drove the Bergerons' cart up to the medical office and guided Cara inside. She wasn't particularly warm toward me, but she wasn't in a combative mood. She was clearly shaken up, but I could tell she was playing along with my examination so she could get some sedatives out of it. However, this time, she genuinely needed something strong to take the edge off. She had just survived a murder attempt by someone she'd thought to be missing. I sympathized with her. I never thought George would willingly come out of the forest.

"Here you go," I said gently, handing Cara a pill and a paper cup of water. She swallowed the tablet and clutched the cup between two shaky hands. I reached deep into the freezer, digging past the bottles of liquor and ice cream bars that Max must have stashed in there when he was the interim medic, and pulled out an icepack, wrapped it in a towel, and handed it to her to hold to her injured throat.

"Try to remember to ice it," I said. "It'll help with the swelling and pain. I don't think you have any serious internal injuries. If you're still in pain when it's safe to travel to the island, you might want to see an ENT, just to be sure he didn't cause more harm. How does your head feel?" I asked.

"It's fine," she said, reclining back onto the exam table.

I pulled out cotton swabs and rubbing alcohol and gently swiped over each scratch. She winced at the first few, but after a while, she remained completely still as the liquid stung her skin.

"How are you feeling now?" I asked after a few minutes of silence.

"Better," she said.

I gave her a kind smile. The medication was working. Finally, she stopped trembling and her muscles appeared to soften.

"That must have been scary," I said sympathetically. "Perhaps you weren't close, but he was still someone you trusted, right?"

She nodded, her eyelids growing heavy. "I thought I could trust him," she said drowsily.

"How often do the two of you spend time together?" I asked.

She thought for a moment. "I'd talk to him a few times a week to make sure everything in the dining room was under control. I never thought he could hurt me. I thought he was obsessed with me."

"Maybe he is," I suggested. "Maybe it's his obsession that led him to try to harm you. Do you think he's capable of harming anyone else?"

She shook her head. "No, I don't think so."

"What about the waitress who fell off the cliff?"

"The drunk girl?" she asked. "I doubt it. I'm sure she just drank too much and fell."

"Did you know Amy?"

"Who?" she asked.

"The waitress who died," I explained.

"Oh, no, I didn't know her."

That seemed evident. I wasn't surprised that Cara didn't even know the deceased girl's name.

"I'm sorry about Sebastian," I said, changing the subject. "I haven't talked to you since. Have you been doing okay?"

"Sure, sure," she slurred.

"I'm sure his loss was very hard on you. Were you close?" I asked, pretending that I hadn't caught them in the act before.

"Yes, we were close," she said casually. "Everyone talks about him as if he was a saint." She giggled.

"Was there something people didn't know about him?"

She gave me a wry smile. "No, he was an open book. He was a bit of a dumbass, though."

I raised my eyebrows in surprise. In the days since his passing, I hadn't heard a bad word about him.

"Oh, you met him. You're not surprised. Daniel is the brainy one. Jamie is the sensitive one."

"What was Sebastian?"

She closed her eyes for a moment. "The fool. I liked him very much, but I think if he were smarter and stronger, he'd be here today."

I blinked a few times, trying to follow her train of thought. "What do you mean?"

Before she could answer, Jamie rushed in.

"Is she okay?" he asked.

"She's fine," I said gently. "I gave her a sedative, so she's going to be kind of out of it for a little while. Keep an eye on her until it wears off, okay?"

"Okay," he said, helping her off the exam table. He wrapped his arm around her and started walking toward the door. I wanted to stop him and talk to her for a little while longer, seeing as she was finally willing to speak with me for the first time since I'd arrived on the island.

But I wasn't sure how reliable her testimony was under the influence. She seemed so certain about things she couldn't possibly know. She was adamant that Amy was drunk and fell off the cliff, though she didn't even know the girl. She thought that George had a dangerous obsession with her, though no one had mentioned it in interviews. Then, she thought that Sebastian had died from his own stupidity when everyone else regarded it as a tragic incident. How could she possibly know any of those things for certain? It was possible that she was giving me shit because she hated my very presence on their perfect little island. Or she truly knew something that she wasn't willing to share with the rest of us.

CHAPTER TWENTY-THREE

The next morning, I saw Cara on her morning walk as I made my way to George's makeshift jail cell. She wore big, dark sunglasses and had tied a silk scarf around her neck. She looked fashionable, but I knew she was trying to cover up nasty scratches and bruises.

"Good morning," I said warmly, walking to her side of the walkway. "How are you feeling today?"

"Fine," she said coldly. "Have you talked to George yet?"

"I'm going to do that now."

Her mouth puckered into a scowl. "It's going to be a waste of your time. He has problems telling the truth."

"Really?" I asked. "I hadn't heard that about him."

She looked over my shoulder as if she were

counting down the seconds until I would leave her alone. Last night, I had seen a different side of her. She was gentle, vulnerable, and open with me. Now, she was back to her cold, stuffy self. I don't know what I did to upset her when I got to the island, but if she wasn't high on sedatives, then she was nasty toward me.

"Well, if you need anything, make sure you come by the office."

"I'll be seeing a specialist when I'm allowed off this godforsaken island. I don't think you're exactly qualified to be doling out medical advice."

I wanted to say a whole bunch of rude things to Cara, but I held my tongue. Her husband was technically my employer, and I needed to make it off the island with a fat check in my hand. But that didn't stop me from thinking about how I'd given her too much sympathy the previous night.

"See you around," I said, faking kindness. In return, she turned up her nose as she walked past me. I wasn't sorry for our conversation to end.

It had just started to rain as I grabbed my apple and plain bagel for breakfast. Drops dotted the stone steps leading down to the outdoor buffet. By the time I finished my meal, my shirt was damp.

"Excuse me," I said awkwardly, peeking my head into the kitchen.

"What can I do for you?" a chef asked, wiping her hands on her towel.

"Is George still in the storage cellar?" I asked quietly, trying not to cause a scene.

She nodded wordlessly and gestured toward a door with a lock dangling from the latch.

"Three-seven-four-eight," she whispered before walking away. Once she was out of sight, I grabbed a paring knife and tucked it into my back pocket. Then, I picked up a large blueberry muffin and a poured a large glass of orange juice.

"Hey, George, it's John," I announced as I set my food offering in front of him. He sat on a giant burlap sack of basmati rice, a scowl on his face. His kitchen whites were covered in dirt and grass stains, and a five o'clock shadow coated his face. He looked a mess and none too happy to be locked in a dark and dank cellar.

He remained silent. I hadn't known George for long, but every time we spoke, he was downright chatty.

"I heard you're not talking to anyone."

"This is the first food I've gotten since I was put in here," he said. "It's hard to talk when your mouth is dry."

He chugged the glass of orange juice, then stuffed the top of the muffin into his mouth. It was a grotesque display, but I couldn't blame the guy. He didn't look like someone who had ever skipped a meal, let alone three.

"But you'll talk to me, right?" I asked. "I thought we got along pretty well."

"Can you bring more food?" he asked.

"Sure," I said. "What do you want?"

He thought for a moment before answering. "Get me a plate of fried chicken, mashed potatoes, green beans, and two cans of cola."

I frowned at him. "You assaulted a woman. I don't know if that makes you deserving of a special feast. Besides, it's because of your involvement in this whole mess that most of the food had to be thrown out."

He looked sadly at his feet. "You're right. I would appreciate it if you got me whatever you could. I'm so hungry and dehydrated I can hardly think straight."

"Sure," I relented. "I'll round something up for you."

I carefully backed out of the room and spun the lock before going off in search of his demands. Feeling as though I shouldn't be so kind to a criminal, I grabbed a silver serving platter and grabbed a bottle of water, a wilted salad, and half of a tuna salad sandwich. Then, realizing that a satisfied George would speak more than a cranky and hungry man, I snagged a packaged snack cake and a warm can of cola from a pallet in a storage area. I reset the combination lock and returned to find him exactly where I'd left him.

"This is all I could find," I lied. "It's still morning, so the lunch food isn't out yet.

"Oh, thank you," he said, taking a bite out of the sandwich. "Yes, this is good enough."

I tried to think of a good starting place. I didn't know whether to start with his sudden evasion or the attack behind the Bergeron cabin. I knew that interrogations were tricky, and the subject could clam up if I didn't go about this right.

"Do you have any injuries from the incident?" I asked. "Maybe I can bring some supplies back later," I suggested.

"Does it look like I was in a fight?" he asked, his hands reaching toward his battered face.

"You've got a black eye and some scratches," I admitted.

"I don't feel so hot," he said gruffly. "I always thought Jamie was a nice guy. He really beat the crap out of me. I wouldn't be surprised if I have broken ribs. I just hope I don't have any more serious injuries."

"Well, I suppose I could bring you ice and ibuprofen when I return," I said hesitantly. "I treated Cara last night and saw her just a little bit ago. Don't you want to know how she's doing?"

George gritted his teeth and looked away from me.

It almost appeared as though he were remorseful, but he could have also been afraid of the consequences of nearly murdering the owner's wife.

"How is she?" he said so softly, it was nearly a whisper.

"If your grip were any stronger, you would have crushed her windpipe and killed her. Alternatively, if Jamie hadn't been there to stop you when he did, she would have died of asphyxiation. Either way you spin it, you're lucky that you'll only be charged with assault or attempted murder, rather than murder. Your sentence will be much shorter. Plus, if you get a good lawyer and your record is clean, you'll probably get out on parole before your time is up. Prisons have kitchens, you know. You might get to keep your career."

Tears welled up in his eyes. He cracked open the bottle of water and washed down the lump in his throat.

"But she's okay now?" he stammered.

"Sure, she'll recover. She's in pain and you scared the shit out of her, but she'll survive. Her bruises look about as nasty as yours."

He nodded and took another drink. Now that he was softening around the edges, it was time to start gathering some information.

"When we talked the other day, you spoke very highly of Cara," I said, frowning. "I guess I don't understand what happened. You seemed so eager to help me out, but then you ran away when I asked you a simple question. Can you help me understand? I like you, George. Despite your actions, I don't think you're a bad person. Should I?"

"No," he whispered. "I'm not a bad person."

"See?" I smiled. "I knew I should be able to trust you. Now, why did you run? You know that makes you look suspicious. If I can understand, maybe I can help you out."

He shook his head. "I don't know. It was stupid of me. I just got scared when you guys came in and started saying stuff about poison in my food. I swear I had nothing to do with it. Why would I want to hurt anyone?"

"You hurt Cara."

"I think I lost my damn mind in that jungle. I just wanted to come back to the resort so I could get something to eat and drink, then get on the first boat out of here. I wouldn't mess with food. As a chef, that's just something you don't do."

I nodded along, trying to show that I was listening intently to his ass-covering.

"Here's the thing I don't get," I said innocently. "Why didn't you explain that to me when we first found the pong-pong seeds? I would go so far as to say we were pals before all of this. I ate your food and it was damn delicious. You let me sit and chat while you worked. When I came in and asked you who'd special-ordered the seeds in the curry, then the jambalaya, why didn't you just tell me? You wouldn't have been in any trouble. You could save lives, you know. You'd be the hero."

A single tear slid down his cheek. "I don't want to talk about this anymore. I'm tired."

I sighed and rubbed my sunburned neck. "Fine. I can give you a break. First, can you just tell me why you attacked Cara? Were you upset because her husband yelled at you yesterday?"

He shook his head. "I just wanted to get out of this place. She was in the way. I feel terrible that she had to get hurt, but she would have stopped me."

"Right," I said, starting to feel like a confession was on his way. I didn't want to push him too far too soon. With the storm building strength, he wouldn't be able to leave the cellar for a few days at the very least. Eventually, the isolation would get to him and he would say anything just to keep me around for company. I didn't like using these methods, but they were at my disposal, and frankly, there wasn't much of a choice.

"Enjoy the rest of your lunch, George," I said, already feeling drained. "I'll stop by later if you're interested in talking."

When I left the kitchen, the rain had picked up. I

ran back to the medical office, but by the time I arrived, I was soaked. Since no one was around, I wrung out my shirt in the sink and hung it up to dry. Then, I lay on the exam table and tried to think of reasons for an innocent man to run.

I knew he was hiding something, but I was getting the feeling that he had less to do with the murders than his actions suggested. He committed a violent crime against a woman, but he seemed so sorrowful and remorseful. He wasn't a cold, calculating criminal. He'd done something terrible, but I couldn't completely point the finger of blame at him. There was more he wasn't telling me. However, I couldn't tell if he was hiding out of fear of getting caught or out of fear of being harmed for disclosing a secret.

I played around with different scenarios for hours but never reached a conclusion. I just had to occupy myself until the next meal time so I could bring a food offering in exchange for information. I had never experienced such a slow day as the resort medic.

Finally, I received a call that someone was having a medical emergency in the kitchen, though I wasn't given any specifics about who it was or what the injury was. Assuming it had something to do with cuts or burns, I stuffed some extra gauze and suturing equipment into my kit and ran toward the kitchen.

When I got there, I saw a few guards mixed in with

the kitchen staff in a huddle, but no one was doing anything. Once I managed to push past the crowd, I realized they were standing in front of the open door to the cellar.

My heart dropped upon the realization that something had gone terribly wrong with George. Immediately, my mind went to suicide, but I couldn't remember seeing anything dangerous in the cellar. Then, I feared that he'd managed to hurt someone else.

"What happened?" I asked, pushing to the forefront of the commotion. There, I saw George, facedown in a puddle of vomit. I flipped him over and checked for breathing and a pulse, but there were none. I started chest compressions, thinking that I might be able to revive him, but eventually, I realized that his body was cold. After a few minutes, I stopped and looked back at the guards. They looked as puzzled as I did.

"We came in to check on him and give him some water," one said, looking baffled. "He was like that when we opened the door. I don't know what happened."

"I believe you," I said warily. "Please, can I have everyone return to work?" I said, raising my voice.

"Do you want me to find Jamie and Daniel?" the guard asked.

"No," I said after a moment of thought. "I'll speak

with them later. If you could, I'd like you to keep anyone from entering this space, please."

What I didn't say was that I didn't want the Bergerons around the crime scene. Whoever was committing these murders was getting personal, and I didn't want the family of the last near-victim to be contaminating a crime scene.

"Actually," I said, changing my mind once I remembered how quickly rumors spread, "just have someone find Max and send him here. I want a second opinion."

CHAPTER TWENTY-FOUR

"I'm starting to feel like John Watson," Max mumbled as he crouched down beside me. We had built a small barricade of tables around the entrance to the cellar so we could have some privacy as we examined the scene. "This is really too bad. I liked George."

"I did too," I mused. "I mean, for the short time that I knew him. I just talked to him about four hours ago too. He wasn't in high spirits, but that was understandable."

"You're thinking suicide?" he asked.

I shrugged. "He had a secret that he didn't want to share. I'm not ruling it out."

I checked his pockets and found nothing but his resort ID. I was hoping that I would find the pong-pong seeds in his possession . . . unless he had swallowed them. I glanced at his vomit and didn't see anything that resembled the poisonous plant, though it would be hard to tell without a more thorough analysis.

"Looks like foul play," Max said, pointing a finger at George's bruised face.

"That was Jamie's handiwork," I replied. "All of those injuries were pre-existing. He was sore when I talked to him this morning, but not in serious pain."

"Can we rule out internal injuries?" Max asked. "Sometimes, the internal organs can bleed or leak nasty stuff without localized pain. I'm sure his head hurt after getting the shit beat out of him. Maybe it was a brain bleed."

"No, we can't rule it out," I said, thankful to have Max to discuss all the possibilities with me. I was clearly biased in this case. "But what's the old saying about hearing hooves?"

"You think it's the poison," he concluded.

"Shouldn't I?" I asked. "It's an identical death. I'm sure he suffered in the last hour, but no one could hear him from down there, especially during the lunch rush. It gets loud and hectic in here."

I listened for a moment and heard the sounds of clattering pans and voices shouting directions. If I shouted out, I wasn't sure if anyone would hear me. Plus, he could have been weakened from the poison and unable to produce the same volume that he might have when he was well.

"I'd agree with you," Max said. "Are you counting this as the fourth homicide?"

I exhaled sharply. Things were getting out of hand very quickly.

"Yeah, I think so. Am I out of my depth here?"

Max pursed his lips. "Does it really matter? The police can't get here anyway."

"Good point. I'm just not sure how far to go. Do I recommend that everyone stay in their rooms until the police can safely get here? The employees have got to be freaking out by now. I'm starting to get a little concerned."

"Let's take a step back," Max said, reminding me to relax and focus. "How could he have possibly been poisoned? What did he eat?"

Looking around the storage cellar, I mostly saw food that needed to be prepared. Bags of rice and beans sat in one corner of the tiny space. Shelves contained dented cans of ketchup and mustard. Dusty bottles of wine lay flat on a wooden rack. Other than that, I couldn't find any opened packaging. It didn't appear as though George ate anything that was in the cellar before he'd arrived.

Since he told me the guards didn't feed him, I

knew that they weren't responsible for the poisoning. The only food he ate was the meal I delivered.

My stomach sank at the thought of being the one to hand over the deadly poison. Had I been made a part of this murder plot?

Max was quick to reassure me. "If you did give him poisoned food, how would you have known? What exactly was it?"

"Juice, a muffin, salad, a sandwich, a packaged cake, water, and soda. Three of those things were in unopened packages. The others were fairly bland. What could have possibly been poisoned?"

"Beats me," Max said.

I combed back over the food items, hoping to discover that something went unfinished, but to no one's surprise, George had devoured everything, not even leaving a crumb. If it weren't for the obvious pattern of mysterious deaths, I might have called it a heart attack. The coroner's office certainly would.

I rolled the empty soda can back and forth in my hands as I tried to think. Then, I noticed a clear sticker on the can. I pulled it off and saw a droplet run down the side of the can. I dropped it immediately and made my way up the stairs.

"Where are you going?" Max asked, startled by my sudden movement.

"I have to go to the medical office," I said hastily. "I need to check on something."

"What do you want me to do?" he asked, throwing his hands in the air.

"Find Daniel and Jamie and let them know about the death, but advise them to stay clear of the body."

"What, exactly, do I tell them?"

"Whatever I told you," I said from the top of the stairs. "I'll talk to them later."

I walked briskly back to the medical office, planning each of my steps in my head before I got there. Once inside, I closed and locked the door behind me.

While people spoke about Dawn's wild reputation, she was a meticulous recordkeeper and highly organized. When I arrived for my first shift as resort medic, I remembered seeing a clipboard with an updated inventory of supplies and corresponding lines where used supplies could be notated in an effort to keep an accurate count of the things she had in stock. I assumed she used this so she could reorder supplies before she ran out, as the shipments could take days to be delivered, but now I saw a more useful meaning.

In my hours of boredom, I continued with her system in hopes that my mindless counting could help the next medic. So, I recalled the supplies I used with each patient and updated the clipboard. Now, I would use it to confirm or dismiss a hunch I'd had since holding the suspicious soda can.

According to the count, there should have been forty-seven syringes on hand. When I counted the ones in the drawer, I only found forty-four.

I inhaled sharply. I feared I was correct in my suspicion. Someone stole syringes right from underneath my nose and used them to poison the soda that killed George.

Then, the implication of the poisoning finally hit me. I had been the one who'd pulled the can out from a cardboard flat. No one could have possibly known that I was going to pull that soda to give to George. That meant that it wasn't a targeted attack at all. The killer was trying to poison whomever they could. George just happened to be the unlucky one who'd opened the can.

I didn't know where to go first—the kitchen or Daniel's office. Concerned about minimizing risk, I returned to the kitchen for what felt like the tenth time that day. Luckily, when I arrived, every can on the flat was accounted for.

I must have looked like a madman as I pulled out each can and examined every surface. Shockingly, every single one was intact.

I was starting to wonder what was really going on. How could I possibly take the only tampered-with can out of the whole thing? It was the first one on the left corner, but still, what were the chances? I felt like I was losing my mind. If I had picked up any other can, George would still be alive. In fact, he would probably have already spilled the beans already, and things could have gotten back to normal.

Feeling shaken, I went to join Max at Daniel's office. The two of them were deep in conversation, tense looks on their faces.

"Where's Jamie?" I asked.

"Cara's having a rough day," Daniel said with a slight eye-roll. "She insists that he stay with her. I suppose things are different now that George is dead."

"I'm afraid so," I muttered.

"Do you know what killed him?" Daniel asked.

I sighed. I couldn't help but feel guilty for delivering the poisoned drink at his request.

"His can of soda had been tampered with," I admitted.

"Now we have to worry about packaged foods and drinks?" Daniel asked, his eyes nearly bulging from his head.

"I think I took care of it," I said. "I checked every last can in that flat. They were all untouched. I think he drank the only one."

Daniel frowned. "How can you possibly explain that?"

I opened my mouth to speak, but I hadn't quite

found the words. "Honestly, I have no idea. Bad luck, I guess."

Daniel sat back in his chair and closed his eyes for a second. "Well, we can kiss this company goodbye," he concluded. "I don't see what other choice I have besides just shutting the whole place down. People will lose their jobs and I'll lose everything, but we can't have another death. What are we meant to do when we can't even eat or drink things in sealed packaging?"

"I think if you sent out a memo for kitchen staff to check for tampered packaging, it'll be fine. I understand your concern, though. I'd also suggest once the storm clears up, you get rid of everything and start fresh with new supplies."

"I'll get on that," Daniel said. "Honestly, I've really lost my appetite. I don't foresee myself eating much of anything until this clears up."

"I'm trying my best," I said, realizing I sounded like a child. "I'm committed to catching whoever is doing this."

"Thanks," Daniel mumbled. "Now, if you'll excuse me, I need to make some calls."

Max and I ducked out of the office and exchanged a silent look.

"Join me for dinner?" I asked Max. "I never thought I'd see the day where two medics were necessary for meals, but here we are. I'd like an extra set of eyes on our diners."

"You got it," Max said. "Until then, I'll be drinking from glass beer bottles."

He had a point. I couldn't think of any way the poison could be introduced into glass.

Before dinner, I walked around the premises in the rain, my borrowed umbrella swinging wildly as I navigated the slippery paths. I walked past the luxury cabins, hoping to catch a glimpse of Cara. After all, she had been my last patient. I thought back to our brief time together and tried to remember a moment where I might have looked away from her for a while. I couldn't quite recall such an instance, but I also wasn't expecting her to take anything from me.

At dinner, I ordered vegetable barley soup and a bread roll. As I chewed each bite, I watched the other diners. I was surprised to see Cara sitting next to her husband. She was still wearing the scarf around her neck but had removed the sunglasses. She must have been a whiz at makeup, because I could hardly see the small scratches that lined her face.

I tried not to make it obvious that I was primarily watching her, but she was now my prime suspect. When I thought about it, she was one of the few people at the resort who had a connection, no matter how small, to each of the victims.

Dawn had been sleeping with both her husband and her lover. If that wasn't enough of a reason for her to poison Dawn, I don't know what was. I wasn't exactly clear on why she would want to kill Sebastian, but she was obviously sleeping with him—not to mention, she told me that he'd died of his own stupidity. Maybe she tried to break it off and when he didn't agree, she got rid of him.

While she didn't claim to know Amy, they were still connected. If Cara was indeed that mastermind behind the poisonings, she'd used Amy as her pawn to retrieve the poisonous fruit. Poor Amy was likely upset about her role and willing to confess to her part, which would have screwed Cara over. It was easy to get rid of her while the girl was drunk and walking along the cliffs.

Then, there was George. While I wasn't sure if this death was intentional, George and Cara were friendly to each other. I assumed that Cara was the one who'd made a special order, convincing George that the seeds were meant for one person. Somehow, he went along with it, either through his blind love for Cara or his stupidity. Once he realized he'd had a hand in the deaths, he fled. When he realized that Cara was still a threat, he'd tried to take her out.

That was my working theory, at least. There were still some holes in the motive that I couldn't fill. My mind kept going back to how devastated she had been while Sebastian lay dying on my table.

Cara and Jamie appeared to be in surprisingly good spirits. Cara actually had a smirk on her face instead of the scowl she usually wore. She kept leaning over to whisper into her husband's ear. A few times, he laughed loudly in response or leaned over to kiss her. He appeared to be fairly intoxicated, which seemed to be the norm as people around him continued to die. From what I could tell, Jamie seemed to have a very hard time dealing with loss.

After dinner, I nursed a beer straight from the bottle with Max as I began to fill him in on my most recent suspicions. He was surprised, but he was eager to accept Cara as the villain, as he had never really liked her in the first place. Still, we had a hard time understanding what would drive her to kill each of the victims.

Eventually, Jamie got up from the table alone and stumbled away from the dining area. Instinctively, I got up to speak with him. I had stepped no more than ten feet off the patio when I heard retching coming from the bushes.

"What did you drink tonight?" I asked frantically.

"Rum and Coke," he gasped as he vomited into his landscaping. "I think I overdid it."

"I think you should come with me," I said, grabbing him by the arm.

By the time we got to my office, Jamie was in bad shape. He held his stomach and groaned while alternatively getting up to vomit into my sink. His face was pale and his pulse was fast. It was all too familiar.

"I need you to do exactly as I say," I instructed as he clutched his stomach and rolled into the fetal position. I dug into my cupboard and pulled out the parcel from Carlos. After quickly reading the instructions, I filled a syringe with the clear liquid and injected it straight into Jamie's vein in the crook of his arm.

"What's that?" he asked, too weak now to fight me off.

"Poison antidote. I don't know if you heard this, but George died from drinking poisoned soda. You didn't drink too much tonight. You were poisoned."

"How?" he moaned. "Am I going to die?"

I exhaled. "No, you're not going to die. I caught you in time. You're going to be fine. However, I need you to pretend as though you're dying. I think I can catch the killer that way."

He nodded, taking a few labored breaths. "You just want me to pretend I'm dying? Do I need to do anything else?"

"No, exactly that. I want the killer to think they're

getting away with it. I think they'll let their guard down."

"Are you sure I'm not going to die?"

I placed my hand on his shoulder. "I'm sure. The antidote will take a little while to work, but you're going to feel much better very soon. I need to make sure this doesn't happen to anyone else. I don't have much of the antidote left and there's not much time. Stay here, make yourself comfortable, and if anyone comes up here, act sicker than you really are. I'm talking about your wife, your brother—anyone. Do you understand?"

"I understand," Jamie said weakly.

"I'll be back as soon as I can," I said before running back to the restaurant. When I hit the patio, I tried to act natural. I casually approached Max and clapped him on the shoulder.

"Jamie's been poisoned, but he's fine now," I said softly. "I think this is our chance to finally catch our person."

"Really?" Max said, sitting up a little straighter.

"Yes, and I need your help. Don't let on like anything is wrong. We're going to have to watch everyone here like a hawk. Plus, we need to go through every bar and serving station and look for tampered soda cans."

"Anything else?" he asked, his eyes wide.

I quickly glanced over my shoulder at Cara, who was still smirking.

"If anyone gets sick, send them to the medical office as quickly as possible. I'm not sure how many of us will get the chance to cheat death tonight, but I'm going to try like hell to keep everyone alive."

CHAPTER TWENTY-FIVE

I followed Max to a small shed off the main walkway to the kitchen. He lifted the garage door to reveal cases of every type of alcohol imaginable. In addition to the booze, there were flats of beer and sodas stacked four feet high. We had our work cut out for us.

Under the fluorescent light, Max and I pulled out every single can, running our fingers up and down the sides for signs of tampering.

"Is it really this easy for people to gain access to all areas of the resort?" I asked.

"Well, we go where we please, don't we? For the most part, the average guest keeps out of employee spaces. The regulars move freely about the resort."

"So I'm right in assuming that Cara could get in here without anyone batting an eye?"

"I'd say so," he replied, stacking cans in the corner. "No one seems to notice that we're in here now."

I pushed the poisoned cans into the open section of the shed. After digging through a few flats on the top, we had discovered twelve cans that looked suspect. The part that concerned me the most was that they were randomly distributed. Someone had taken a lot of time and effort into making the attacks random. Basically, the killer was in full control of the resort, poisoning food and drinks as they pleased. Only they knew which meals to avoid in order to stay alive.

"What do we do with these?" Max asked. "Destroy them?"

I bit my lip. Though I didn't want anyone to get their hands on the poisoned soft drinks, I also wanted some evidence to prove that there was something serious going on at this resort. I feared that someone with wealth and power, like the Bergeron family, could downplay the murders. I needed the police to know that this was very serious. We were dealing with a spree killer in a confined space.

"Do you want me to tell Daniel what we've found?" he asked.

I hesitated to respond. "Not just yet. I want to make sure that he can be trusted. Until then, we have to protect the resort on our own."

He sighed. "That's a tall order. Do you really think he might have something to do with this?"

"I don't want to make the wrong call," I replied. "People do strange things when family is involved. I've seen cases where battered spouses will defend the other, even after they beat the shit out of them or tortured them for years. I've heard of family members supporting disgraced business people after a bad scandal. Even if the crime is reprehensible, people will stand by their family members. I guess it's hard to go against the people you're closest to, even if they've done something wrong. I don't understand it, but I've also never been in the position to defend someone close to me."

By the time we had searched the top six flats, we had accumulated fifteen tainted cans. I found an empty box and started piling them inside, hoping we could preserve some fingerprints for proof. Unfortunately, neither of us were wearing gloves, so our prints were all over the cans as well.

As we made our way down the stack, we found that the highest concentration of tainted sodas were located at the top. I imagine the job became tedious after a while when we searched two rows that were completely clean.

"Do we give up?" Max asked about the same time I was asking myself the same question.

"I–I don't know," I said hesitantly. "Maybe we should be thorough. There are lives on the line."

"This is going to take a while." Max grunted. "Shouldn't someone be keeping an eye on Cara? Eventually, she's going to go looking for her husband, right? What's she going to do in the meantime?"

I nodded, gritting my teeth with worry. "Can I ask you a favor? Can I leave you here with this task while I make sure everyone is still alive out there?"

Max grunted. "Fine. You owe me."

"More than you'll ever know," I replied before bolting from the shed. I quickly walked through the patio, but the Bergerons had already left.

"John!" little voices called. I jumped, not expecting anyone to notice me. I saw Fantine peek out from behind a tree, her brother close behind.

"What are you guys doing?" I asked, trying to make my voice sound calm and cheery.

The kids stood side by side in matching rain jackets. "We can't find Jamie," Fantine said.

"Oh, I think he has some important work to do," I said, not wanting to tell the kids that their guardian was very ill and recovering from an attempted murder. "Maybe you should go back to your rooms and hang out. There's a storm coming."

"We've been in bad storms before," Toby replied, feeling grown up at age ten.

"Of course you have," I said softly. "Well, I'm sure Jamie will come talk to you guys later."

"We're bored," Fantine said. "Should we see if Miss Cara wants to play with us?"

"No," I said quickly, forgetting how much Cara disliked the children. They were just as at risk as anyone else on the island. It would be too convenient to get the problem children out of the way. After all, they had partially become her responsibility. I had no doubt that Jamie had written the kids into his will. It would be too easy to trick the children into ingesting the poison seeds in something sweet, and without Jamie there to protect them, I worried that was exactly what Cara would do next.

"I'll play with you," I said hastily, checking our surroundings. "We're going to play detective,"

"How do we play?" Fantine asked, looking a little skeptical.

"The first rule is, no one can see you. No one can know that you're playing the game. If you get caught, then you lose the game. Do you understand?"

They both nodded. They were bright children, and I had no doubt in their ability to spy. However, they did not know how serious this operation really was. I hoped they wouldn't blow our cover because someone of authority had crossed their path and asked too many questions.

"Now, I want you to hide by the kitchen. I just want you to watch the people go in and out of the kitchen. Try to remember who you see. Do you know all the cooks and wait staff?"

Toby nodded.

"Good. Now, just watch and don't let anyone see you. If you see anyone who doesn't work in the kitchen try to enter, come find me and tell me what you saw."

"Okay," Toby said, looking a little excited.

"Now, Fantine," I said, turning to the girl. "I want you to do the same thing, but hide outside the medical office. If you see anyone try to enter the building, I want you to come find me."

"Okay," she responded, looking a little more enthused than she did before.

"Now, if something happens and you feel scared, you can come find me. Do you understand the rules?"

They both nodded.

"Good. Now, go to your posts. I'll find you when the game is over."

They both took off running into the darkness. I felt a little guilty about tricking them into helping me catch a killer, but I was running out of options. I just really hoped that no harm would come to either of them.

My phone started ringing, so I frantically dug it out of my pocket to answer it. My nerves were buzzing with fear and anticipation. I was just waiting for a call from Max to tell me that someone was sick with pong-pong poisoning. Instead, the caller ID told me that Marcie was trying to reach me.

With my heart still racing, I tried not to laugh with exasperation. Here I was, on a private island with a murderer, about to solve the case I had thrown myself into for a week, and my ex was calling me, likely because I had cut her off from my money. I couldn't believe it.

Truth be told, there had been a time early on in the breakup that I'd considered meeting up with her once the case was solved. I didn't like to cut people completely out of my life, and I thought it might be best for the both of us if we could step away with a clean break. That way, she could try to explain herself and I could let her know how hurt I was by her cheating.

Now, I had seen how crazy a crazy partner could be. One day, you're having a disagreement about the house or the kids your spouse wants to adopt. The next, you're committing multiple murders. While I didn't think Marcie was capable of killing, I knew she was capable of hate and scorn, and I didn't want to be on the receiving end of it.

I didn't have time to talk, nor did I want to. Instead,

I went into my contacts list, blocked her number, and then deleted it. With that out of the way, my mind felt a little clearer already. Now, I could fully focus on my case without her lurking in the back of my mind.

CHAPTER TWENTY-SIX

My priority was now to watch Cara. With the restaurant and my office covered by two precocious twins, I felt a little safer tailing her. I wasn't sure if I could stop another murder, but I was fairly confident that I would be able to ensure that my prime suspect was covered. Not knowing where else she'd be, I walked to her cabin and lurked outside.

It reminded me much of the nights I'd spent watching cheating spouses. Sometimes, I'd sit across the street from a house, just waiting for a couple to get home from an outing. I'd climb over fences, bribe yappy dogs with treats, and peek into windows, just to get the confirmation I needed to collect my money. Sometimes, the only thing that separated me from the criminals was intent. I lied, sneaked around, and invaded people's private spaces to prove that their lives weren't as perfect as they made them out to be. In the end, someone had justice, but no one had peace. Someone always got hurt.

I watched through the window of the cabin and saw Cara slip off her standard heels and slide into a pair of house slippers. She walked into another room and reemerged into the living room a short moment later, now with a silky robe fastened over her clothes. As she settled down into the couch, I marveled at how calm she seemed.

Then, she pulled out a hand mirror and began to inspect her neck, carefully touching the bruised skin. Once she was done with her examination, she pulled out a bottle of expensive-looking cream and rubbed it into the skin, and all the while, her husband lay in the medical office, suffering the effects of a deadly toxin.

At the very least, I felt as though she should be looking for him. After all, he left the dinner table looking green around the gills, and I wouldn't be surprised if someone else heard him retching just outside the dining area. It had been over an hour since I had treated him, yet Cara hadn't begun to look around for her missing husband. Was she waiting for something, or was that just part of their regular relationship dynamic?

By now, she had the TV on and her phone was in

front of her face. I didn't get the impression she was planning on going anywhere anytime soon. For now, I felt safe in that she wouldn't go out and purposefully poison anyone. It just looked like she was waiting for the pong-pong seed to do its job.

So, I left my spot behind the hedgerow that surrounded their bungalow. I had some doubt plaguing my deduction skills and I needed to clear up a few loose ends before I started making accusations.

Daniel's cabin was about fifty yards away from his youngest brother's. Sebastian's sat vacant between the two. I felt a chill go up my spine as I walked past the home of a man I had watched die.

Feeling a little nervous, I knocked on Daniel's door, realizing that I had never seen him relaxed. I had spoken to the other brothers while they had been under the influence, but my meetings with Daniel had always been business. He looked surprised when he opened his front door, a glass of clear liquid in his hand.

"Where did you get that drink?" I asked.

He furrowed his brow. "From my personal bar," he said, gesturing to the metal cart on the wall. It held a glass bottle of vodka and a plastic bottle of tonic water. From my brief assessment, it didn't appear as though it had been tampered with.

"Can I help you?" he asked, perplexed by my sudden intrusion.

"I have some questions," I said, feeling adrenaline race through my veins.

"What kind of questions?" he asked.

"Business, mostly," I said. "Is this a bad time?"

He scoffed. "It's a bad time, but not in the way you mean. Please, have a seat. Do you want anything to drink?"

"I'm fine," I said, instinctively refusing a cocktail. Sifting through hundreds of soda cans will do that to a person.

"What do you want to know?" Daniel asked. He looked more exhausted than I had ever seen him.

"What's going to happen to your resort without your brother?" I asked. "Will you split his share with Jamie?"

He shook his head. "We haven't really discussed it," he replied. "Sebastian wasn't the hardest worker, but he knew his stuff. He handled most of the finance stuff. Honestly, I'm kind of clueless without him here. Sometimes, I just get so frustrated because his death has made a mess that only he could really fix."

"Really?" I said, surprised by his remarks. "I was under the impression that he wasn't the intellectual type."

He frowned. "Where did you get that idea?"

"I don't know," I lied, thinking about Cara's remarks on the middle brother.

"He wasn't serious about much, but he was a good business partner. I can hire a new CFO, but there's no guarantee that they'll know as much about our business as he did."

"What about Jamie?" I asked. "What does he do around the resort?"

"Well, right now, he's working on making the place more sustainable. When he started his greenhouse project, we thought it would be useful to grow fresh food to use in our meals. It's expensive to power a resort on an island, but his goal is to make our resort the first fully self-sustained resort in the world. Not only would it bring in eco-conscious consumers, but in the long run, we'd save so much money. He's really taken the initiative to get a good start on it."

"That's impressive. So I guess you could say that your brothers are an invaluable part of this island."

"Of course," he said, looking at me as though I had asked a silly question. It seemed to me that there was nothing for Daniel to gain by losing his brothers. In fact, it seemed as though he could lose his dream business without them.

Unless Daniel was a master actor, I highly doubted that he had anything to do with the murder plot. Not only did he appear to dislike his sister-in-law, but the bond between him and his brothers seemed genuine. He cared about them like an older brother would, but he also relied on them to keep their family business running. He could seem cold and detached sometimes, but I couldn't find a reasonable motive. Still, I continued to test the waters, just to make sure my instinct wasn't wrong.

"Do you know where your brother is now?" I asked.

He frowned. "At home? At the greenhouse? Why?"

"Does he have a normal nightly routine?" I asked casually.

He thought for a moment. "I guess he usually checks in on the kids before they go to bed. If Cara's in a good mood, he'll come up to the cabin with her. If they've been fighting, you can find him in his greenhouse, drinking. That's the closest thing to a routine that I can think of."

"Do you know where Cara is?" I asked.

Daniel sat up a little straighter, and a deep crease lined his forehead.

"Why are you asking me this?" he said softly.

"How was your brother when he left dinner?"

"Drunk, but that happens from time to time. He and Cara were all over each other. I would have sworn they were on something, but Jamie and I swore not to use any drugs after Dawn died. That's when we thought she'd died of bad drugs. Is there something wrong?"

"No," I said firmly. "Jamie is fine."

He continued to stare at me with his dark eyes. "Why do I feel like you're hiding something?"

I took a deep breath. I was the one who was supposed to be noticing lies, not him.

"I believe that your brother was nearly killed tonight," I said, my voice calm. "When he left dinner, I followed him on a hunch. I worried that he might have been slipped something. As it turns out, he had. He got extremely sick, just like all the others had. I gave him a high dose of the poison antagonist and he's resting comfortably in the medical office. He's going to be fine."

Daniel covered his mouth and nose with both hands. He closed his eyes and took a few slow breaths. When he composed himself, he placed his hands back on his lap and looked me directly in the eye.

"Who did this?" his voice rasped.

I bit my lip. "I don't have proof yet, but I suspect it's his wife."

I could see the muscles of Daniel's square jaw clench. His eyes blinked as he tried to piece the puzzle together, just like I had been doing for about a week now. He looked stumped, so I tried to help him along my line of reasoning.

"She poisoned Dawn's food because she was sleeping with Jamie. I think that's the easiest one to understand. George let her into the kitchen and allowed her to do whatever she wanted. She had the authority, plus George was vulnerable to flirtation. I'm not exactly sure why she killed Sebastian, but while she was under sedation, she said that Sebastian died from his own stupidity. That's why I thought he didn't do much around the resort. Now, I can see that her statement doesn't really make sense."

Daniel blew a puff of air from his nostrils, practically fuming like a dragon. "She must have been referring to his weakness. You'd have to ask a psychologist, but I think my brother had what many people might call a sex addiction. He was very intelligent, but he couldn't control himself when it came to women. He'd get himself in trouble by sleeping with the wives of our guests. I had to allow management to give out free rooms and entire stays just to keep the guests from causing a scene and tanking our business. When he had the urge, there was no controlling him. That's probably what she was referring to."

"Then it's possible that she got jealous of his sleeping with other women," I suggested. "Then, there's Amy. Amy was the one who took the fruit from the pong-pong tree."

"She knew Cara's secret," he interjected. "Knowing Cara, she probably acted all fake and tried to be this girl's friend. I bet she took her to the spa, got her drunk, then made sure her death looked like an accident. That's something Cara would do. She can spot weakness in a person and exploit it."

"You seem to have some bad personal experiences with her," I noted.

"We've never gotten along. Now, how about George? She wouldn't have visited him."

"No," I said. "That was a chance killing. Max and I have been going through your food stores tonight and have removed many cans of soda that have pinholes in them. I think she injected cans at random. The sugary ones cover up the bitter taste. When mixed with alcohol, I doubt anyone would taste the bitterness."

"Why, though?" he asked, shaking his head in exasperation.

"Spite?" I suggested. "Maybe she's just trying to make it look like the killings were all random. Finally, we have your youngest brother. I overheard them fighting one night, and they were arguing over Sebastian."

"Really?"

"Yep. He said that she probably wished that Sebastian were alive and he were dead, and she did not refute that. Now, I'm wondering whether Sebastian's meal was supposed to go to Jamie that night."

"They did fight a lot," Daniel admitted. "Jamie confided in me when they had marriage problems. I just can't believe that Cara would try to kill Jamie."

"You can't?" I questioned, wondering if I had gone wrong somewhere in my reasoning.

"I mean, I can, but the thought is just so terrible." He groaned. "She's lived down the road from me for years now. All along, I was having dinner next to a murderer. She's always been a pain in my ass, but this is extreme."

I could tell that Daniel was having a hard time accepting what I was telling him. Even I was having some difficulties connecting the dots in places. But this was his family I was talking about. As an outsider, it was easy for me to come in and notice things that someone else might not. I could pick at his seemingly perfect family and find the problems. I could see motives and accuse people he had known for much of his life. I could say the horrible things that no one even dared to think about.

Having said everything I had in my theories, I worried that I had disclosed too much. I could tell Daniel was in shock. I was forcing him to sit down and deal with all the horrible truths about people he cared about. I wouldn't be surprised if he went into denial. From there, he would probably thank me for my effort and send me back to the mainland. It wouldn't be wise, but I would understand. Maybe the police would step in and close the place down and arrest someone. I wanted Daniel to listen and believe me, but I didn't necessarily expect him to.

"What are you thinking?" I asked after a long silence between us.

"I don't know what to think," he replied, his voice low.

"Your brother is sick, but he's fine. I've instructed him to stay put until I return to check on him. I have a feeling that Cara will eventually go looking for him. When that happens, I don't want her to know that I'm suspecting her involvement."

"What do you want me to do to help?" he asked.

I raised my eyebrows. "Do you believe me?"

He nodded solemnly. "I do. And I want to help end this once and for all. What do you need me to do to make that happen?"

I resisted smiling. Having Daniel's approval meant a lot to me. He was an intimidating man and I hated asking him for help.

"Things are peaceful at the moment. Cara's home and it doesn't look like she's getting up anytime soon. Now, I need you to corroborate my hunches. You know more about these people than I ever will. So, I'm going to need to know everything that will pin her to all these murders. Are you willing to do that?"

"Anything," he said.

"Good," I replied, pulling out my notebook. "Let's get started."

CHAPTER TWENTY-SEVEN

"This isn't easy for me to do," Daniel said nervously. "I'm generally a pretty private person. I'm the one who keeps the family drama swept under the rug."

"I get that," I said, mustering as much compassion as I could. "Believe me, I have no interest in salacious family drama. I just want to know why Cara would kill people at the resort. Is this a sudden change in character for her?"

Daniel scoffed. "I mean, none of us would have pegged her as a murderer—that's for sure. I remember meeting her years ago, and I didn't really care for her then."

"Why not?"

He took a second to find the right words to describe her. "On paper, she's the kind of girl anyone like us would want to marry. She came from a good family, she's educated, she's hot, and she has a bit of a wild streak in her. The first time Jamie brought her home to meet the family, she put on a good show of being the perfect girlfriend. She talked sports with my dad and gave my mom interior design advice. She flirted when she spoke to any of us boys and pranced around in cute outfits. She was everything she was meant to be."

"What's not to like about that?" I asked.

He looked at the ground. "I could tell it was phony behavior. I was older and more experienced. Jamie was still in college and so enamored by the pretty girl who was interested in him. I still maintain that he could have gotten anything, but she was the president of the hottest sorority on campus, the queen bee. She made him believe that she was hot stuff. Little by little, I watched her loose ends unravel. She would get really bitchy about stupid stuff."

"Like what?"

"Oh, one time, Jamie and Cara planned to go out to a new club. She had bought a new dress and was excited about showing off at this opening. That afternoon, my grandma had a stroke, and of course, we all went to see her in the hospital."

"And she was angry about that?"

He chuckled. "The nurses actually told her to leave the room because she was so pouty about having to be there for my sick grandma, who passed away a few days later. She whined and cried the whole time we were there, trying to say goodbye to a dying grandparent."

"Jeez," I said under my breath.

He nodded in agreement. "That's the kind of girl she is. She's totally self-obsessed. She could be okay one minute, but then the next minute, she's throwing a tantrum."

"And Jamie chose to marry her, even when he must have known these things about her?"

"Again, he was young and naïve. All around him were friends proposing to their future trophy wives. That, plus my parents' dismay that Seb and I had never settled down, must have made him think it was the right thing to do. And to give her some credit, she is capable of making him happy from time to time. Unfortunately, she's even better at making him miserable."

"So why didn't they split up?" I asked, trying to count the years they had been together.

"I tried to convince my brother that he'd be better off that way. He already spends so much time away from their home just to stay sane. He'd lose half of everything he has, but I think it would be worth it. He's worried that it's too late for him. He wants the traditional family life. Sometimes, I think he'd be better off paying a boatload for a lawyer to help him adopt the twins."

I felt my heart sink at that remark. I was only a few years older than Jamie. If he was too old to have a chance at a good family life, then it certainly wasn't going to happen for me. I'd never thought much about having the whole wife, two kids, and a two-story house thing, but the thought of not even having that option made my stomach twinge.

"I mean, the fact that she's been sleeping with her brother-in-law is grounds for divorce as it is. I was angry with Sebastian for doing that. He should have been able to tell her no, but like I said, he just wasn't capable of that. At the very least, I told him to be discreet."

"I saw them going at it in a cabana," I admitted.

"Exactly." He groaned. "You know, she even tried to come onto me a few times. Of course, I turned her down. I'm protective of my family. I guess I'm not protective enough, or my brothers wouldn't have been poisoned."

"Well, if you never suspected Cara was capable of such a thing, I don't know how you could have stopped it," I said reassuringly. "What did Cara say when she tried to come onto you?"

"Oh, she just talked about how jealous it would make the other two. One day, she heard from Jamie that I was annoyed with my brothers for not having my back at a particularly rough staff meeting. She thought I'd want to get back at them by having sex with her. When I turned her down, that only made things worse. Every now and again, she'd get really mean and tell me that I was impotent if I didn't sleep with her."

"Really?"

"I don't think she can comprehend that someone might not want to have sex with her. She uses her good looks and her sexuality as weapons to get what she wants."

"That's why George liked her so much and allowed her to do what she wanted in his kitchen. He must have known that he had done something wrong. Maybe he tried to strangle Cara because he knew that he was powerless against her."

"Seems reasonable," he replied. "It's probably the same reason she poisoned Sebastian, though sometimes, it seemed like she liked him more than her own husband."

There was a sadness in his voice, one of regret. He poured the remaining droplets of his drink into his mouth, then got up to pour another one.

"You know, I tried really hard to help my youngest brother," he said with a sigh. "My parents always told me to watch out for him. I put a lot of time and energy into helping him. You know, I'm horrified that this is how things went, but is it wrong that I feel a little relief? Finally, we can get her out of our lives forever. It's not going to bring Sebastian back, but at least we can save Jamie. Do you think you have the evidence we need to get a conviction when the police finally manage to get here?"

I chewed on my lip. "God, I hope so. I did the best I could to preserve evidence, but it's hard when there are hundreds of people walking around, messing with everything. In a normal investigation, I imagine that the whole place would be shut down. Everyone remotely near a crime scene would be wearing gloves and probably even protective suits and booties. I won't lie to you, I'm a little concerned that she'll be able to get a really good lawyer and may get a lesser charge."

He grimaced. "I've thought about that too. However, when the police came to investigate Amy's fall, they ruled it an accident. And everyone thinks that Dawn and my brother died of heart attacks. How do we know they wouldn't screw up this investigation?"

"I guess we don't," I said.

"I know this probably goes against protocol, but I'm glad that you're here, even if you're unable to conduct an investigation like the police. Even if we can't get her locked away forever, at least we'd be able to file a civil suit. She has my brother's money, but with any luck, we can maybe get some out of her and start a trust fund for the twins. I think that's the last thing she'd ever want."

I smiled. "That sounds like a perfect idea. I hope we can get some justice."

"Me too," he said softly.

We sat there in silence for a few minutes. I hadn't realized that we had been talking for almost an hour. I wondered what Cara was up to. I had planned on keeping a close eye on her but got sidetracked while taking notes about her behavior.

"I think I'm going to make sure she's still at home," I said. "Then, I'll probably go check on Jamie to make sure he's comfortable. He probably needs some extra fluids to flush all the poison out."

"I'll be here," he said sadly, swirling ice cubes around his glass.

I left Daniel's cabin feeling terrible for the man. He had so much responsibility on his shoulders. Not only did he have to make sure the resort was running smoothly, but he also had to watch over his adult siblings and ensure that their private lives were in order.

I walked in the grass on my way to Cara's cabin, just in case she was on high alert. I was surprised to find that the lights were now off. It was still too early to go to bed, especially if one's husband was missing. I walked up to the window and peeked inside. From the light coming from the nightlight near the door, I could see her house slippers by the rug.

Fearing she had slipped out without my knowledge, I quickly came up with an excuse to speak with Jamie. I rang the doorbell, then knocked loudly when that didn't bring her to the door.

I swore under my breath and ran straight back to Daniel's house. I burst through the door without knocking, fearing the worst of Cara's disappearance.

"She's not home," I sputtered. "I lost track of her."

Daniel got up and wordlessly retreated into a bedroom. I heard a drawer open and close. When he returned, he was holding a small silver handgun.

"Jeez, man," I said, surprised by the weapon he was holding.

"Relax," he muttered. "I don't want to take any chances. If we catch her trying to poison anyone else, I want to be prepared. No one on this island is going to die tonight. I let shit go too far, and I'm going to suffer the consequences. This ends tonight."

The gun made me nervous. I preferred hand to hand combat whenever the situation called for it. There was something about the battle of strength and savvy that felt more just to me. Anyone could fire a gun, and guns often left the suspect unable to tell their side of the story when everything was said and done. However, Cara was unpredictable, and if Daniel thought this situation called for his pistol, then I deferred judgment to him.

"Where do you think she is?" he asked.

"I have no idea," I replied. "She's clearly not interested in her husband's condition. The last she saw him, he was just outside the dining area. She has no way of knowing that I practically dragged him to the medical office and saved his life. Maybe she's checking in on her poisoned drinks to make sure they were distributed."

"And maybe she is looking for Jamie around the resort," Daniel suggested. "I'm sure she's been rehearsing for her role as the grieving widow."

I cringed. "You may be right. Let's start at the dining area. I also want to see how Max is coming along with his search. I'm worried that he could become a target."

"He's always stood up to her," Daniel replied. "I could see how that might piss her off."

We walked in darkness, the wind whipping at our faces. A few times, I thought I saw someone lurking in the shadows, but I figured that was just my nervous imagination at work. When we got to the shed, Max was wrapping a cardboard box in duct tape.

"I got them all," he huffed. "Every last one of them. Where do you want me to put them?"

I looked at Daniel for his opinion. He looked horrified that his stores had become tainted so easily, right under his nose. For someone who took great pride in his hand in the business he owned, he didn't look very good at that moment.

"Shove them in that back corner," he said. "I don't want anyone to accidentally find them. When the storm clears up, we'll submit them as evidence."

Max pushed the box into the corner of the storage garage and covered it with other boxes, effectively hiding it. He wiped his hands on his shorts and gave us a satisfied smirk.

"Now, where's the action?" he asked.

I looked at Daniel. "I'm not sure. We're going to look for Cara. Maybe it's best if you go around to all the bars and make sure there aren't any tainted cans lying around."

Max shook his head in defiance. "Have you had a look around? None of the bars are operating. There's a hurricane coming and no one wants to be outside at the moment. The only place serving booze at the moment is the beer hall, and unless you can stick a needle through a keg, no one's getting poisoned down there."

"Maybe it's worth a check," Daniel suggested.

"Nah," Max said, "I'm coming with you. I want to help find that bitch—no offense, Daniel."

Daniel rolled his eyes. "Do you think I'm going to take offense? She killed my brother. I ought to kill her."

I raised my eyebrows and eyed the gun in his back pocket.

"But I won't," he continued, sounding tired. "I just want this to end."

"Then what are we waiting for?" Max smiled. "Let's hunt her down like she hunted down our friends."

I could feel excitement buzzing between Daniel and Max, but for some reason, I just felt dread. Cara had managed to outsmart us for over a week. How did we know she wouldn't do it again?

CHAPTER TWENTY-EIGHT

B y now, the self-doubt was starting to creep in. I was an inexperienced private investigator leading a very serious homicide investigation. I had made an accusation against the wife of a resort owner and had now created a lynch mob of sorts to make a citizen's arrest. The authorities were far away and couldn't reach us if they tried.

If I made a mistake or even just a slight error in judgment, everything was ruined. I didn't even know the law well enough to know if what I was doing was even legal. Cara had a vendetta against me from the start, and I feared that I could be charged for false imprisonment if I didn't do things by the book. Unfortunately, I didn't know what the book said about this kind of situation.

While Cara and the rest of the Bergerons could

afford the best lawyers to handle the ensuing lawsuits, I could not. If Daniel ended up paying me what he offered, I'd be able to put a deposit down on a new condo. I wouldn't be able to pay for a lawyer and support myself throughout a lengthy trial. I would probably earn such a bad reputation as an investigator that I would have to quit my job and go back to being a paramedic. It wasn't ideal, but it would pay the bills.

I hadn't even been working at my new vocation for very long, either. I saw the looks that people would give me when I told them about my career change. They were interested in detective work because of all the fun and sexy movies and shows on the subject, but I could tell that people doubted my ability to suddenly solve mysteries. Then, when I told them about the cases I actually worked on, I watched as their eyes glazed over and their minds wandered. There was nothing sexy about lurking outside someone's house for a few pictures. I was the glorified paparazzi for the average guy.

The weight of what I had gotten myself into pressed upon me with full force. People counted on me to make sure no more deaths occurred and justice was brought to the victims. Too many lives had been lost and too many futures had been cut short. I didn't get the chance to get to know any of the victims very well, but I felt their absence every time I passed by the kitchen staff, read notes in the medical office, or spoke with a surviving brother. I couldn't make any mistakes, but I wasn't skilled enough to do the job as it should be done. Instead of calling in an experienced police force, I had a retired doctor and the resort owner flanking my sides as we went in search of the prime suspect. I had a sick victim in my office, pretending to be dying in case the killer showed up. Worst of all, I had two innocent children acting as my eyes and ears. I would be devastated if harm came to them because I wasn't skilled enough to do their job for them.

As we rounded a corner, I felt a hand pull at mine. I jumped and shook off the weak grip.

"John," Fantine hissed. "I have to tell you something."

"What is it?" I asked, my heart racing.

She pursed her lips and looked around. She stuck out her finger and beckoned me to come closer. I knelt down to her level and let her cup her hand to my ear.

"Miss Cara is by your office," she whispered.

I stood up quickly, and the blood rushing from my head made me momentarily dizzy.

"Good work," I said. "You guys won the game. Now, find your brother and go to your room. I'll give you a prize tomorrow."

She beamed and skipped away, her shoes flapping on the pavement.

"What was that about?" Daniel asked.

I shook my head. There was no time to explain. "Cara's going to see Jamie. Do you have your radio on you?"

Daniel reached onto his belt loop and pulled out his little walkie-talkie. I carefully twisted the knob to get the transmitter on the right station.

"She's coming your way," I said softly but clearly. "Do you know what you need to do?"

"Got it," Jamie's voice echoed. "Play dead."

I tucked the walkie-talkie into my front pocket and looked at the other two. "We need to go to the office," I said. "I don't know for sure, but I'm worried that Cara's going to try to kill your brother—again."

Daniel's hand went toward his back pocket. I cleared my throat.

"We need to be smart about this," I said. "We have no idea whether she's armed or what she might be armed with. I wouldn't be surprised if she convinced security to allow a weapon through the check for her. We can't afford to be rash."

"Jamie? Are you in here?" Cara's voice softly cooed from the walkie-talkie. I grasped at the radio, shocked to hear her voice coming from the other end.

Jamie moaned in response. I could hear footsteps approach him.

"What happened, Jamie?" she asked, no hint of distress in her voice.

A smile came to my face. "That's brilliant," I muttered. "Let's go," I said to Daniel and Max as I held the radio to my ear. "When we get to the office, stay put. I think she might confess."

We walked briskly to the medical office, my legs taking me there on autopilot. I had made the trip from the kitchens to the office so many times in the past week, I was pretty sure I could get there with my eyes closed. I was so engrossed in the conversation happening there that my body was moving without any attention from my brain.

"Are you sick?" she asked. "Do you think you'll make it?"

Static crackled in the background. I could hear the soft crunch of paper and the muffling of the blanket I had covered Jamie in when Cara sat down beside her ailing husband.

"You know, we managed to fulfill our wedding vows," she said nonchalantly. "I know it doesn't make much of a difference to most people, but I think it's better this way. After all, no one wants to be a divorcee. It's messy and there are lots of lawyers involved. We'd only fight over every last cent, and everyone's dirty laundry would be hung out for the world to see. But now, I can take it all and finally live the life I wanted in the first place. It's a shame I didn't get the chance to wipe all three of you off the earth. No, the second that storm clears up, I'm going back to the mainland. I'll buy a nice outfit for your funeral, collect your estate, then leave this godforsaken island for good. I think France will be nice this time of year."

I looked over at Daniel. He was so angry that veins were starting to pop out of his forehead. I couldn't let him in the office with her.

"Your resort will have to shut down. I'm not sorry about that. I know it was your dream, but it was a stupid one. You could have owned this thing from afar, but instead, you made me live here with no expiration date. Now, I'm finally free. You have no idea how good that feels."

By now, we were right outside the door of the medical office. I motioned to Max and Daniel to stand back. Then, I reached for my phone and pressed the *Record* button on my audio recorder as I held the microphone up to the door.

"Why?" Jamie moaned. "You love me."

"I tried to love you, Jamie." She sighed. "I really did. I thought you were the one for me. Back when we were in college, you were so sweet to me all the time. You treated me like a princess. When we got married, I thought we could live that way for the rest of our lives. Then, we came here. You started working and no longer had time to pay attention to me. I stayed at home like an animal in a cage. I tried to take on some responsibility here, but it wasn't enough to keep me entertained. Then, you started sleeping with that nurse, and that really broke my heart. She wasn't even that good-looking. How did you think I'd feel to find out that you were sleeping with someone worse than me? Still, I was expected to be the dutiful wife and stay by your side."

"You cheated on me," Jamie mumbled, his voice weak and hoarse.

"Well, what else was I supposed to do? I got bored being here all the time. Sebastian appreciated me. He'd invite me over on nights that you spent tinkering around in your little greenhouse with your servant kids. You loved them more than you ever loved me."

"Take care of them," he croaked.

Cara laughed a high-pitched cackle. "Are you kidding me? The second they bag up your body, I'm having those kids deported back to their home. They don't belong here any more than I do," she said. "I'll let them have a good meal before they go, but they're not getting any of my money. I earned this. I spent years by your side, making sure you got everything you wanted. I put on a brave face and went to all of those family gatherings I never felt a part of. I made your house into a home and made you look like a respectable man. Your brothers were a terrible influence on you. They should have been able to set an example for what a husband should be."

I looked back at Daniel again. His hands were balled into fists. I raised my eyebrows at him to remind him that he needed to stay silent for the confession to be heard.

"You ruined my life, and now I'm afraid I'm going to have to end yours. Everything is ready to go. The life insurance has been submitted, customs knows that there are two little kids living here illegally, and I've been house shopping for apartments in New York."

Jamie mumbled something that I couldn't understand. I was very impressed by his acting skills. He sounded as though he were in agony.

"Does it hurt?" Cara asked, her voice a little softer.

"Yes," he gasped.

Now, I heard rummaging through drawers. I tried to figure out what she was doing through the sounds I was hearing, but I didn't know the office that well.

"What are you doing?" he grunted.

"I'm showing you a little mercy," she said. "This should help with the pain and make it easier for you to go. When you close your eyes, know it will be for the last time."

This was my cue to intervene. I swung open the door to find Cara with a loaded syringe in her hand.

She opened her mouth in shock, then broke down into hysterics.

"There you are!" she screamed. "I've been calling for help. I found Jamie like this and I didn't know what to do. I think he's been poisoned."

"What are you doing with that?" I asked, pointing to her hand.

She dropped it as though it were red hot. "He's in so much pain. I didn't know how to help him. I've been calling for help for ten minutes now."

I frowned. "I have a radio right here. I didn't get a call. Where's the office radio?"

She looked around the room, her eyes falling on an empty charging dock.

"I've got it," Jamie said, popping up from his reclined position. He looked a little queasy, but much better than he looked when I last spoke to him.

I thought Cara was going to faint on the spot. Her eyes kept darting back and forth between Jamie and me, then at Daniel and Max once she spotted them in the hall.

"It's over, Cara," I said gently. "We know every-thing. We know about the pong-pong in the spicy food. We know you injected it into the soda cans and we've removed them all. We don't really understand why you did it, but you'll have time to explain. Now, if you'll cooperate with us, you won't be harmed. "

I reached out my hand to her, hoping that she would find that her reign of terror was over and just give up. She looked at it for a second, pondering her surrender. Then, she glared at me with bared teeth and grabbed a heavy metal cart with supplies on it. She thrust it forward with all of her might, hitting me square in the shins. I doubled over, trying to regain my balance, but my shoes were tangled underneath the plastic wheels.

That was all the time she needed to slip out the far window, hop down from the office, and disappear into the darkness. When I got to the window, lightning illuminated my surroundings for one brief flash, but there was no sign of her.

CHAPTER TWENTY-NINE

D aniel wrenched the walkie-talkie out of my hand and turned the dial in one smooth motion.

"I need guards around the perimeter," he screamed into the radio. "If anyone sees Cara Bergeron, grab her. Don't let her get into the forest."

I had never seen Daniel so fired up before. It almost frightened me until I realized that having a murderer on the loose was more concerning. I felt like an idiot for letting her get away. She was nearly within reach, and she disappeared in a matter of seconds. Perhaps the most frightening thing about this woman was the fact that no one saw her capabilities. Her in-laws couldn't foresee her homicidal streak, and I'd underestimated her physical strength and speed. She was not just a trophy wife who stayed at home all day and read magazines. She was a frightening criminal.

"Max, find the twins and make sure they're safe," I demanded, feeling sick at the thought of any harm coming to them. He nodded and waddled out of the office and into the night.

"What do you think she's going to try to do?" Daniel asked, looking hopeless.

I automatically looked toward Jamie. I had worked on her modus operandi, but he had lived with her for ten years. He knew her better than anyone, which was apparently not much.

"I–I don't know," he sputtered. His face looked pale and I could tell he still wasn't feeling well. "I don't know where she could go. I can't imagine she'd go to the forest because she hates that kind of thing, but then again, there's nowhere else for her to hide."

"I don't think she thought she was going to get caught," I mused. This wasn't an uncommon trait in psychopaths. They always think they're so much smarter than everyone else that it comes as a shock when they get bested. Given her lack of empathy for anyone at the resort, it wouldn't surprise me if she were one.

"No one is going to sleep until she's caught," Daniel said. "This has gone on for far too long. She's fucking crazy and we're all sitting ducks with her around. She's going to burn this place to the ground."

"Well, if the guards have the perimeter and Max is with the kids, then we're going to have to search the rest. There will probably be a few bakers and prep cooks in the kitchens and someone will be at reception. We'd hear from someone if the whole resort were on the lookout for her. Where's somewhere she would go where no one would bother her?"

"Maybe she went to the house?" Daniel suggested.

I shrugged. "We can start there. Do you have a key in case she locked herself in?" I asked Jamie.

"We have a keypad," he replied. "The code is 2272."

"Let's go," I said to Daniel. Jamie sat up a little straighter, but I could tell it was taking all of his energy just to sit up.

"Maybe you should stay here," I suggested. "We might have to do some running and you're clearly not up for it. We'll keep in contact with you. Keep the radio nearby."

He nodded weakly. I reached into the refrigerator and pulled out one of the drinks we gave to the hungover crowd.

"Well, shall we?" Daniel asked, a grim expression on his face. Together, we walked out onto the path. Small lights illuminated our feet and sparse streetlights cast a glow from overhead. Cara could have been around any corner or behind any bush, and we wouldn't have known. As we walked to the cabins, I found myself constantly looking over my shoulder.

The house looked empty, but I wasn't about to assume that darkness meant there was no one inside. I punched in the door code and flipped on the lights.

"Cara," Daniel boomed. "Stop this. You really don't have to do this."

"You take those rooms," I suggested. "I'll check these ones. Be thorough."

I crept past the dining room toward the master bedroom. Everything was perfectly in place, probably due to the housekeeping staff. I peeked into closets, pushing past rows of dresses and jackets. Dropping to my knees, I searched under the bed with a flashlight. I even opened cupboards under the sink just in case she had contorted herself around the pipes. When I returned to the living room, Daniel was there, shaking his head.

"She's not here," he said, looking as though he was about to fall apart. "I know it's an island, but there are a lot of places to hide. Do I need to send the house-keeping staff out on the search? Do I send the cooks, armed with knives? I don't want to put my staff at risk, but they're kind of already at risk if she's still out there.

What if she's hidden more poison and we just haven't discovered it yet?"

"We'll find her," I said reassuringly, though the words were empty. "I think I have an idea of where she might be."

In the distance, I could hear guards communicating among themselves, though I couldn't hear exactly what they were saying. I could tell that they were just as confused as we were.

"Let's look in here," I whispered, pointing to the greenhouse door. It seemed to me that Cara was on a vengeful tear through the resort, and destroying Jamie's hard work might be something she'd do. That, and I was worried she'd restock her supply of poison before she disappeared again.

The instant I stepped into the greenhouse, something felt terribly wrong. Instinctively, I marched toward the pong-pong tree and found Cara sitting underneath, casually taking a bite out of the poison fruit.

I froze in shock. I had worked so hard to solve the case and bring justice to the deceased, and here my killer was, ending things on her own terms. I couldn't let her do that. I reached into my pocket and held the walkie-talkie up to my lips.

"I need you to open the big cupboard by the sink and find the big vials of medicine and a syringe," I said softly. "Bring them to the greenhouse as soon as you can."

At the sound of my voice, she lazily looked over to Daniel and me, then back to her fruit.

"This thing tastes awful," she said. "At least none of the others could taste it when they ate it. I'm not the monster you make me out to be."

"Drop it, Cara," I said with authority. In response, she took another casual bite.

"If I had any of my oil-extracted poison left, I'd add it to a Cosmopolitan," she said. "That would have been the perfect way to go out—besides a boat, you know."

"Stick your finger down your throat and get rid of it," I said firmly.

She shook her head. "That won't work. Remember, I tried that with Sebastian, but he still died."

I frowned. "What do you mean?"

"That plate was never meant for Sebastian," she said, looking at me like I was an idiot. "I thought you were a good detective."

"Then who was it for?"

"Jamie, obviously. I wanted Sebastian around. Sebastian didn't want Jamie around, though."

"What the hell are you talking about?" Daniel growled.

"Sebastian wanted me all the time. He didn't like the

fact that every night, I went home to his little brother who didn't even want me. But I made it clear that I would not get a divorce. If he wanted to have me, Jamie had to go."

"You're lying," Daniel said. "Sebastian wouldn't have had any part in this."

"No?" She giggled. "Maybe if you weren't such a control freak and took the time to pay attention to your family members, you would know them better. Oh, it's delicious to see you mess up, Daniel. You're such a know-it-all, but you couldn't see everything that was happening under your nose."

I tried to refocus our energy on getting concrete answers. "You're saying that Sebastian was in on the plot to kill Jamie the night he died?"

She smiled. Luckily for us, she was so pleased by her plan that she couldn't shut up. "That's exactly what I'm saying. After I killed Dawn, Sebastian figured out it was I who'd planned her death. After all, I was the only person on the whole island who hated that slut with a fiery passion."

"There's no way he knew," Daniel said.

"You don't give him enough credit." She chuckled. "He absolutely knew. He asked me, point-blank, after she was found. I told him that if he kept my secret, I would make it worth his while."

My mouth dropped open. "I saw the two of you

fighting not long after I arrived on the island. You were in the cabana. Was that about Dawn?"

She smirked. "You saw that? Did you like what you saw?"

"What were you fighting about?" I pressed.

"Oh, he was being a little baby about keeping secrets. He was afraid that I was going to get caught and he would go down as an accomplice. Actually, his real problem was that he got cold feet before I was supposed to help in the kitchen. He made me promise him that we would call the whole thing off. To appease him, I told him it was over and the poison was gone. I guess he never got the chance to figure out that it wasn't over."

"Because you killed him!" Daniel raged.

"It was purely an accident," she said innocently. "After all, I did try to save him. I made him drink that stuff to make him throw up, but too much time had passed. I brought him straight to you, thinking that you could save him."

"Maybe I could have if I had known it was poison," I said, raising my voice.

"I tried to hint at it," she said. "But if I said too much, you would have known that I was involved. My tears that night were genuine. I really didn't mean for him to die, but since I was already too far into it, I had to keep going so I could come out the other side."

She started to take another bite out of the pong-pong fruit, but I snatched it out of her hand and threw it down the pathway in the greenhouse.

"Where does Amy come into this?" I asked. "She was your server that night."

"And she fucked it all up," Cara said emphatically. "I was pissed at her for giving the poison to the wrong person. She had directions to give the special order to my husband, and she chose the wrong man. Afterward, I was worried that she was going to spill the beans."

"Did you get her drunk?" I asked.

"She did that all on her own." Cara smiled. "She must have been a sheltered girl, because she was really freaked out by everything that was happening around here. She was talking about going home because she was scared something would happen to her too. I'm pretty sure she was drinking for the first time, because she had a few gulps of vodka and was blitzed. She said that the other waitresses were drinking because of their nerves too. I told her to take a walk with me and talk about it. She needed to sober up before her shift, anyway. We were by the cliffs when I realized she knew too much and just wasn't smart enough to piece it together. I knew she would talk to someone about the night Sebastian died and you would realize that I was involved. So, it was just so easy to nudge her off the edge. She didn't even scream as she fell. She just wanted to go to sleep."

I was feeling nauseated by how she kept acting as though she'd humanely put people down, like a veterinarian. She seemed to have no idea that these people had lives and wanted to continue living them. She had no connection to anyone and was completely incapable of empathy. As much as I wanted to leave her on the floor of the greenhouse to suffer alone, I needed more answers.

"Why did you kill George?" I pressed on.

She giggled. "I heard that you did. You gave him something to drink and he croaked hours later. No one could hear him beg for help as he got sick."

"You injected something into those cans. Did you do that alone?"

She grinned. "Brilliant, isn't it? I extracted the poison from the seeds and made it into an oil. Then, I carefully injected it into all of those cans. Those awful drinks are so sugary that I figured no one would taste it."

"So it really was random?"

She shrugged. "I guess. Well, I wasn't going to get killed because I don't drink those."

"Why, though?" I asked. "Up until then, each attack was clearly targeted. I assume you spiked your husband's drink tonight?"

She nodded. "That's right. I don't really have a reason besides the fact that someone might trace the deaths back to me. You must think that I'm some kind of monster. I'm just trying to right some wrongs around me. I don't really care about the other people in this resort. If they live, fine. If they die, whatever. It really doesn't make a difference to me."

I heard the door creak open and turned around to see Jamie hobbling toward us with my medical supply pouch. It took great effort for him to move quickly, but he gritted his teeth and charged forward. When I looked back at Cara, she had turned pale. She twisted around, leaned over an empty flower pot, and emptied the contents of her stomach. When she was finished, she turned back around and wiped her mouth, a cool and satisfied expression on her face.

"Bury me in my black Chanel dress," she said dreamily. "I don't care what you tell people about me, but I want to look good when I go into the dirt."

"Why kill yourself?" Jamie asked as he saw his dying wife hold a poisonous fruit in her hand.

"I don't really have any other option," she said wistfully. "I'm sure as hell not going to jail, and I don't think there's any way I can escape this. In the end, I just wanted to come out on top. This is the only way I can do that now. You may still be alive, but your lives will be significantly worse now. The resort will close down. Your precious mistress and brother are gone. I just hope I can haunt you after I take my last breath. It would make all the pain so worth it." She winced as the poison ate at her stomach.

I reached into the bag and pulled out the vial of antidote, then filled a syringe. I nodded at Daniel and Jamie. It was time to end her suffering.

"Maybe we should just let her go," Daniel suggested gruffly. "She's not doing us any good. I don't want to go to trial and see her face. She's already caused enough pain in our family. I say we let her die."

I looked at Jamie. His eyes sank to the ground. He was conflicted.

I wasn't. It was my job to minimize fatalities. I was being paid to track down the killer and make sure they spend the rest of their lives in jail. I didn't want Cara to die, even though she had committed heinous crimes.

When I began to walk toward her, Jamie followed close behind. Even Daniel reluctantly followed suit. Slipping the empty vial into my pocket, I held out the syringe as Cara began to slip into unconsciousness.

"No," she mumbled, trying to fight. By now, she was too weak to get away. Jamie grabbed her hand and exposed the pale underside of her arm. I found a dark vein and injected the last of the poison antagonist into her bloodstream. Then we waited.

"I'm glad Carlos sent me two doses," I said.

"I'm glad we didn't need more than two," Daniel replied.

For a few minutes, we hovered over Cara, silently watching her as the color returned to her face. Her ragged breathing became smooth and calm, and eventually, her eyes blinked open.

"We're going to need some of those heavy-duty zip ties," Jamie muttered as Cara came back to life. Daniel grabbed his walkie-talkie and called off the search, requesting that a few guards come to the greenhouse. Cara tried to fight them off, but she was outnumbered. Her hands were tightly bound behind her back and she was escorted from Jamie's sanctuary.

"Where should we put her?" a guard asked.

"Maybe we should put her in the cellar with George," Daniel suggested darkly.

Jamie winced. "Who would have thought that we would need a jail in our resort? Let's just put her in Sebastian's cabin. The storm is clearing up and we can get her out of here soon."

"Fine," Daniel said, "but I want everyone to stand guard. She's not leaving that house until the police take her out in cuffs."

The convoy of security guards marched a squirming Cara out of the greenhouse and into the storm. Daniel and Jamie stood motionlessly as they watched.

"We're going to have to pay all the guards overtime," Daniel said.

"It's a small price to pay," Jamie responded, sinking down into his lawn chair. He was looking healthier with each passing moment.

"Are you going to be okay?" Daniel asked Jamie.

He nodded but looked at me for reassurance.

"Medically, you're going to be fine," I replied.

"It's going to be a change," Jamie said, searching for the right words. "She was such a big part of my life for so long. I'm a little relieved that our marriage is over, but I still feel lost and confused."

"I know," Daniel said tenderly. "I'm just glad you made it out of it in one piece. I don't know what I would have done if I'd lost you."

Jamie swallowed hard. Sensing I was intruding on a moment between brothers, I stood up to leave.

"If you don't require my services, I think I'm going to wash up and try to get some sleep," I said uncomfortably.

"Oh, of course," Daniel said. "I don't know how we can ever thank you enough for your help."

I laughed to myself. "I'm just glad I could help. I'll check in with you tomorrow."

The brothers gave me an appreciative nod and I saw myself out. As I walked back to my room, I closed my eyes, tilted my head toward the sky, and let the cool rain fall onto my face. I had just solved my first major case as a private investigator. My feelings with completing the task were complicated. I wanted to celebrate, but there was so much sadness surrounding me. For every clue that I gathered, there was a dead person behind it. So many people would never be able to live out the rest of their story, while I would continue to play it out in my head for eternity.

But no matter how many horrors I encountered along the way, I had still righted a wrong on a tiny private island, far beyond the rest of the country's awareness. While four people had died, many more would go on to live amazing lives. That had to count for something.

CHAPTER THIRTY

"Hi, John, how's it going?" Daniel asked warmly over the phone.

"Not bad," I replied as I lounged on the recliner in my new condo. "How are you doing?"

"Just taking it one day at a time," he replied. "I just wanted to call and make sure you received the check."

I glanced over at the stack of mail on my kitchen table. Earlier that day, I had received payment for my services, both by Max and Daniel.

"Yeah, I got it," I said sheepishly. "It's a lot more than we agreed upon."

"Nonsense," Daniel said quickly. "We owe everything to you. None of us would have ever suspected Cara. When Max recommended you, we figured you'd just be testing the purity of drugs. We didn't expect you to find a poison that the coroners and doctors couldn't find."

I smiled weakly. I still felt like most of my discoveries were dumb luck.

"How are things on the island now?" I asked, a whole week after the storm cleared and Cara was taken back to the mainland in handcuffs.

"We're getting back to normal," he said. "We gave most of the staff a paid holiday so we could clear out all the old food and drinks. The people who stayed are getting an overtime bonus, so everyone's happy. Well, everyone is still kind of shaken up, but at least they're all planning on staying."

"That's good," I replied. I was hardly a guest at the resort, but for the most part, everyone who worked there was kind and cooperative with me. I knew that Daniel and Jamie felt terrible for all the fear and pain Cara had caused their employees.

The day after we caught Cara, the storm faded enough for police to come. While she had been very chatty as she assumed she was dying, she clammed up when it came time to deal with the police. I figured since she couldn't get out of trouble by dying, she decided she'd try to get herself through the trial.

The woman from the medical examiner's office looked very sheepish when she came to collect

George's body. I felt a little bad for them because it wasn't their fault they got the incorrect cause of death on three counts. From what I heard from Carlos when I called to thank him for sending the antidote, there are so few cases of homicide by pong-pong poisoning that it would have been seen as irresponsible to check for it. Apparently, it's almost impossible to detect unless you've got a good reason to test for it. When I told the examiner what the three died of, she quietly took my word for it. I tried to be kind, but I was afraid I came off a little holier-than-thou. Perhaps it was because I was mocked when I'd tried to tell people that these healthy people did not die of simple heart attacks.

Though the resort was lovely, I wanted to leave as quickly as possible. After all, I'd only planned on visiting for a day or two. Instead, I was there for over a week. I tried to get on the police boat with Cara, but the head of investigation wanted me to stay and give a full statement. So, I remained another day. Luckily, Jamie managed to bring in some fresh food and alcohol from the mainland, and I finally felt like I could relax.

It was strange talking to the real police after the fact. I understood that I would be unpopular among their crowd as a dinky private eye working a murder case. But I found that for the most part, the detectives I spoke to just wanted to know what happened. I handed over every note and piece of evidence I had. When they were finished with me, they thanked me for my cooperation and sent me on my way to pack and have a few drinks with Max.

"Well, I just wanted to make sure you got your payment," Daniel said awkwardly. "We're working on rebuilding what Cara destroyed, but before long, we'll be back to normal. I also wanted to let you know that if you ever want to come visit, your stay is on us. Just call the front desk and let them know you want to visit, and they'll set you up with the full experience."

"Thanks, Daniel," I said politely. I didn't want him to know that the last thing I wanted right now was a vacation on his murder island. Maybe in the future, I'd have to take him up on his offer.

When I hung up the phone, I grabbed the checks from the stack of mail and hung them up on my refrigerator. Between my payment for that job and the little jobs I began working the day I got home, I wasn't too worried about starting my life over without Marcie. I would be just fine.

No sooner had I returned to my chair than Max called me. I had told him to call me if anything interesting happened at the resort. I called him crazy at the time, but he chose to stay through it all. Nothing could ruin this man's permanent vacation, not even a series of murders. I had to give him some credit for his determination to live the easiest life possible.

"I just talked to Daniel. He didn't say much. Do you have a better scoop?" I asked, curious about how everyone was really doing.

"I know their reservations really took a hit after the paper came out with their story. Did you ever read that one?"

"Yeah. I liked the part where they called me an amateur sleuth," I joked. "I wonder how Cara's doing? I can't imagine prison is good to her."

"She's either manipulated everyone around her to do what she wants, or the other girls hate her and want to kick her ass. Either way, things aren't looking good for her. Jamie told me that the state prosecutors have a really strong case against her, thanks to you."

"We all had a part," I said, feeling embarrassed.

"You can't get much better than a recorded confession. And your testimonial will be worth a lot because you have no connection to this place. The pop cans have her fingerprints all over them. The syringe they found with her poison in it has her fingerprints on it. They have so much evidence that I'm pretty sure she'll get life."

"Wow," I said, though it really wasn't a surprise. She just wasn't the typical criminal I was used to working with.

"Oh, Jamie's adopting the twins," Max added. "It'll be fun to see him parent, though I know he's nervous about being a single dad."

"He'll be great," I said.

"And I forgot to tell you this, but I've accepted a position as medic!" Max exclaimed.

"Seriously?" I asked, shocked that he was asked and that he accepted.

"After this past week, I decided that I liked having something to do. And as you know, it can be a pretty easy job. I've cut down on day drinking and I'm down to just a few beers at night."

"Hey, that's great," I said. I'd doubted his ability to keep everyone at the resort healthy, but the more I thought about it, there was no one better for the job. I was glad that Max had something to do to keep him out of trouble.

"I want you to come out and visit sometime soon," Max said.

"Yeah, I'll come visit eventually," I lied.

By the time I hung up the phone, I couldn't help but feel a little nostalgia about my time on the island. It had been hard work, and I slept very little while I was there, but I did something that I never thought I could do. Within just one week, I had managed to break up and move on after being cheated on by my long-term girlfriend, solve a murder case, and even save a few lives. I no longer doubted my ability to solve tough cases or live independently as a single person. And after everything I'd witnessed on that accursed island, I never wanted to return to my old life.

ABOUT CHASE WATERS

Chase Waters grew up in Miami, Florida and bounced around from one coast of the country to the next. He writes thrilling mysteries that take place near the coasts.

Sign up for his VIP Reader Club and find out about his latest releases, giveaways, and more. Click here!

The Dangerous Coast Of Florida Suspense Series

Dead In The Water - Book 1

Made in the USA
Columbia, SC
16 April 2021